DOPE GODS 2

Lock Down Publications and Ca$h
Presents
DOPE GODS 2
A Novel by *Hood Rich*

Lock Down Publications
P.O. Box 944
Stockbridge, Ga 30281

Visit our website @
www.lockdownpublications.com

Copyright 2020 by Hood Rich
Dope Gods 2

First Edition September 2020
Printed in the United States of America

Lock Down Publications
Like our page on Facebook: Lock Down Publications
@
www.facebook.com/lockdownpublications.ldp
Cover design and layout by: **Dynasty Cover Me**
Book interior design by: **Shawn Walker**
Edited by: **Lashonda Johnson**

Stay Connected with Us!

Text **LOCKDOWN** to 22828 to stay up-to-date with new releases, sneak peaks, contests and more...

Thank you.

Submission Guideline.

Submit the first three chapters of your completed manuscript to ldpsubmissions@gmail.com, subject line: Your book's title. The manuscript must be in a .doc file and sent as an attachment. Document should be in Times New Roman, double spaced and in size 12 font. Also, provide your synopsis and full contact information. If sending multiple submissions, they must each be in a separate email.

Have a story but no way to send it electronically? You can still submit to LDP/Ca$h Presents. Send in the first three chapters, written or typed, of your completed manuscript to:

LDP: Submissions Dept
P.O. Box 944
Stockbridge, Ga 30281

DO NOT send original manuscript. Must be a duplicate.

Provide your synopsis and a cover letter containing your full contact information.

Thanks for considering LDP and Ca$h Presents.

Hood Rich

Prologue

Finesse laid out the last of the fifteen pictures on the table for Javier to see. "Okay, now you need to pay close attention to this power player right here because he is the drug lord that will be looking to come at you from all angles. This older, heavy-set fellow's name is Juan Salazar. He is head of the New Orleans Syndicate. He runs military assault rifles from China back to the United States. He is also connected with the Columbians and the Sinaloa's out of Sinaloa, Mexico. He is a ruthless and cold-hearted individual with no regard for human life other than his own. You must be conscious of him and his crew of like-minded, callous individuals at all times." She placed her hand on his shoulder while she kept her eyes pinned on the pictures before them.

"How do you know all of this?" Javier picked up Juan's picture and zoomed into the man's evil eyes.

"Just like there are a lot of things I don't know about you, but I give you the benefit of the doubt, you must do the same thing with me. You have to trust me. Just know that I have your best interests at heart." She sighed and wished what she was saying about his interests were true. Over the past few months, she'd become quite fond of Javier. He tugged on her heartstrings and made her feel special, that was something she didn't think any man was capable of doing.

Javier looked her over. "I do trust you, and I'ma take heed to everything you are telling me. Now, walk me through all this one more time and break down the connections that report back to Sinaloa. This shit seems like it's really interesting."

"Okay, now if you—" She stopped mid-sentence because there was a knock at the door.

Javier stood up and held up a finger. "Hold on, I already know who this is because I only gave my security permission to let my lil' cousin, Peto, come through. Let me holler at him real quick. I'll be right back, baby." He leaned over and kissed her lips.

"Mmm. Hurry back, honey. We need to get this figured out before you make your next major move." The more moves Javier made up the narcotics' ladder meant the more powerful of a bust she would have when she made it. She could already see the tabloids.

"A'ight, hold on." Javier grabbed his .40 Glock off the table then went and opened the door after seeing Peto standing outside of it. "What's up, lil' cuz? What did you need to holler at me about that was so important?"

Peto looked both ways. He felt his heart beating hard in his chest. It all was all or nothing. He took a step back and pulled two twin Desert Eagles from his belt. "You took my family away from me! Die Javier!" Then his fingers were squeezing the triggers.

Chapter 1

Joaquin jumped out of his Cadillac Escalade and came around the big body of the truck. He stopped in front of Emilia's passenger door and pulled it open. She stepped out of the truck in a form-fitting, white Gucci dress that Joaquin had bought for her only hours earlier. Joaquin held out his hand and took a hold of hers. Together, they marched into the church with sixty of La Perla's loyal savages behind them. Emilia's hair flowed lovely over her shoulders. She looked up to Joaquin and felt butterflies taking over her stomach.

Joaquin held open the door and allowed her to walk in before him. Once inside the church, Father Juarez was already awaiting their arrival. Joaquin led the way and stopped in front of Father Juarez. He turned to Emilia and held her hands. Their savages settled into the pews of the church. The sounds of their shoes squeaking and clothes rustling as they situated themselves were noticeable in the church.

Joaquin stroked Emilia's cheek. He spoke to her in Spanish, "Baby, you already know we are going to do this the right way when the time presents itself, right?" He looked into her sparkling eyes and smiled.

She nodded. "As long as you are going to be my husband, Joaquin, that is all that matters to me. I love you so much."

Joaquin felt his eyes become watery. He took a deep breath and blew it out. "Father, marry us."

Father Juarez stepped forward, blessed Joaquin, and then Emilia. He uttered a few verses from the Bible, then began to go through the ceremony of marrying the two. After ten minutes of the formalities, he finally came to the part that Joaquin was used to hearing. "Emilia Jimenez, do you take Joaquin Peralta as your husband? Will you promise to love him through sickness and in health, for richer or for poor, will you obey him, and stand as his wife for as long as you shall live?"

Emilia nodded her head. "With all that I am, I will." She slid the gold ring on Joaquin's finger.

"And Joaquin Peralta, do you take Emilia Jimenez as your wife? Will you love her, will you cherish her, will you provide for her, and be there by her side through sickness and in health, for richer and for poor, as long as you both shall live?"

"I promise to do all these things and so much more. She is the light of my life." He slid the one-carat diamond ring upon her finger and kissed the back of her hand.

Father Juarez held up his hands and did the sign of the cross over the pair. "Then it brings me great joy to say that by the powers that are in me, and by the grace of Jesus Christ, I now pronounce you husband and wife. Joaquin, you may kiss your lovely bride."

Joaquin picked Emilia up into the air and allowed her to wrap her thighs around him. He kissed her lips, and seconds later, they were tonguing each other down hungrily. The church erupted with applause before the savages hopped up and back on point. Joaquin set Emilia down and looked into her eyes happily. "I love you, Baby. I promise to be the best man for you."

"I trust you, Joaquin. I trust you with all my life." She wrapped her arms around his neck and kissed his lips again. Emilia had never been so happy in all her life. She was wishing that her mother had been there to see her and Joaquin wed, or at least Cecilia. Nevertheless, she was thankful for the moment just the same.

***

Later that night, Joaquin held hands with Emilia while they walked barefoot in the sand along the beach. The waves of the water crashed into the big rocks loudly. It was a hot and humid day. There was a breeze coming off the East that gave the pair a sense of relief. Emilia's hair blew in the dry wind. She looked over and up to Joaquin pulling a strand of hair out of her face.

"Ever since I was a little girl, Joaquin, I've had a crazy crush on you. I was too shy to act on it, but I always said that when I get older, I was going to marry you. Now, look and behold, I've done it. I am officially a Peralta. It's time to get down to business."

Joaquin laughed. "I don't even know what that means, but I used to say the same thing as well. I always said that when I grew up, I was going to marry you and that we were going to have a big house. Now that I have you as my wife, I have accomplished that part. Now, I need to get you the house and the security that you deserve as a woman. Then I want to start putting some babies right in there." He rubbed her stomach.

Emilia smacked his hand away. "I hope you don't think I am ready to lay down and start having kids because I am nowhere near that. I am ready to get on the front lines and fight for the land of La Perla. This is my home, and if my husband is going to be the King of this island, then I am going to be equally as important. It is my birthright."

Joaquin stopped in his tracks. "Emilia don't talk so stupidly. You are a wife now. Why would I allow you to fight in a man's war? You are supposed to be protected and at home. I will do the heavy lifting, and I will stand as a knight over La Perla."

Emilia had to do a double-take before she made sure that Joaquin was standing in front of her and talking the way that he was. She turned her head sideways and jerked it backward.

"If you think just because I have become your wife that it means you can control or muffle me, then you have me sadly mistaken. I am a woman. I am strong. I am determined to fight for La Perla. I refuse to be denied the opportunity to defend my country. I will not allow the establishment to silence me, nor will I allow my husband to do so. Do you understand me?" Joaquin clenched his jaw and tensed his muscles. He looked angrily into Emilia's face for a brief moment, then he became soft for her. "You are going to drive me into an early grave, Emilia." He held her chin and rubbed the side of her face with his thumb. "I would never look to silence, nor prevent you from fighting for La Perla. I married you because I see myself inside of you more than anyone else in this world.

"Nobody loves La Perla more than you and me." He sighed. "Emilia, you are my wife now, which means we are one flesh and one spirit. We are equal. All that I can build for the sake of our people, you can build also. But you are responsible for building it up and fighting from a feminine standpoint. Build up your army of female warriors that are willing to put it all on the line and die for the sake of our land that is La Perla. I believe in you, and I will always have your back. With your lil' feisty self." He pressed his lips to her forehead.

She closed her eyes and smiled. "Thank you for believing in me, Papi. I thought for a minute I was going to have to get all up in your butt. Though we are people of tradition, I do not desire to be stifled like the women before me. I will submit to you out of love, not tradition and fear, and you are supposed to do the same. Also, even though we are warriors, I still think that it is essential that we come fully under God. We are going to need that added protection."

"You just thought all of this through thoroughly, huh?"

"Yeah, so what do you say?" She placed her small hands on his chest.

"I'm willing to do whatever it takes to make you happy. You are my life, Emilia." He pulled her to him and held her close.

***

Martina opened the oven door to her stove and pulled out the pan of baked chicken. She slid it onto the stove and fanned away the smoke. She danced to the music coming out of the speakers of her old school, small radio. She turned in a circle and slid across the floor. She laughed; she could feel her lower back paining her. She placed her hand on it to give her a sense of relief. "Whew. Where did the years go?" she spoke loudly to herself in Spanish.

Pedro stepped into the kitchen with an evil sneer on his face. He eyed Martina with hatred. He took a serrated blade out of the sheath of his knife case. Before becoming a proud member of the San Juan Jackers, Pedro's initiation included murdering the household of Joaquin. Due to a severed tongue as a motive to crossover to the Jackers and to complete the tasks that they requested, Pedro was ready to start with Martina.

I have to get me a dog or something, she thought. *This is the second time somebody has crept up on me.* "To what do I owe this surprise, Pedro?"

Pedro couldn't talk, and even if he could he wasn't in the mood to do so. He flipped the kitchen table and grabbed a hold of Martina. Before she could fight him back, he brought the knife down into her back and twisted it, pulled it out and slammed it into her again. He knocked her to the floor and straddled her body. He then started stabbing over and over again with no regard.

Justina heard the flipping of the table and it woke her out of her sleep. She ran her hand over her face and yawned, stretching her legs out. She rubbed her stomach and slipped out of the bed, neglecting to throw a robe around her bra and panties. She yawned again as she came to the bedroom door and stopped to pull her panties out of her butt. The hefty cheeks had swallowed them. She opened the bedroom door and stepped out of it. She sleepily walked down the hallway with her eyes closed. Every few steps, she would open them to see what was in front of her. She popped them wide open when she got close to the kitchen and heard Pedro grunting loudly while he stabbed Martina's lifeless body over and over for his amusement. Justina stopped in her tracks when the scene registered in her brain. She screamed.

"Oh, my God! What are you doing to my mother?" she hollered.

Pedro stood up and wiped the blade off on Martina's cheek. He looked over Justina's perfect body and became lustful. He stepped over Martina. Justina slowly took in the scene before her eyes, then took off in the other direction. Pedro stood still just glaring at Justina. Suddenly, he took off after her.

***

Joaquin led Emilia back to the Escalade and helped her get inside of it. He closed the passenger's door behind her and walked around to get into the driver's seat of the truck when six black Hummers rolled into the parking lot and stopped in front of him and his crew of savages. Joaquin's men upped their firearms ready to crush whoever was inside of the military vehicles. Joaquin stood at the ready, fearless. Emilia hopped out with both .9 millimeters in her hands ready to die beside Joaquin if the mission called for it.

The lead Hummer's door opened, and Sudan stepped out of it with black war paint all over her face. Her animals came behind her with military issued assault rifles. She held up her hand to keep them at bay. She stepped up to Joaquin and lowered her eyes. "Are you willing to die for La Perla tonight?" As she finished the words, six more Hummers rolled into the lot, and the masked Sudanese killers hopped out of them heavily armed. "If you aren't ready to die for this land, bow down. Now!" she hollered.

Hood Rich

Chapter 2

Peto took a step back and nearly tripped over his own feet. He squeezed the trigger of his gun back to back.

Blocka! Blocka! Blocka!

"You took my family from me, Javier!" He watched his bullets rip into Javier knocking him backward. Javier fell over the couch and wound up in a push-up position. Peto rushed over to him and popped him a final time.

Blocka!

Javier flipped over to his stomach and laid out flat. Peto got ready to flee from the room, almost certain that Javier was deceased. He felt elation and a strong sense of vindication.

Before Peto could get out of the house, Finesse kneeled on one knee and pulled her service weapon from off of her hip. She closed her left eye and aimed.

Boom! Boom! Boom!

Her bullets whizzed across the room and found their home inside of Peto's chest one after the other.

Peto felt the bullets enter into his chest. He took a deep breath and felt his throat filling up with blood. He dropped his gun and took off running with his vision starting to go blurry. He made it to the steps and fell down them. He got outside and his heart began to pound loud in his ears. Blood seeped out of his mouth. He looked over his shoulder to see if he could locate Javier or Finesse, but neither were anywhere to be seen. Peto made it to his awaiting stolen Ford Taurus and jumped inside of it. The ignition was already activated. He threw the car in drive and took off down the street. He only made it halfway before his eyes crossed. He slammed full speed into a parked Chevy Blazer. The front end of his Taurus bent upward. His face shot forward and landed into the horn hard. He spat blood across the windows before he faded away to his death with blood leaking out of him like a strainer and the horn blaring.

Beeeeeeep!

Back at Javier's home, Finesse rushed to Javier's side. Javier stood against the wall holding his stomach. Blood oozed through his fingers. More blood spewed out of the hole in his right shoulder. Finesse grew worried. "Baby, holy shit. You need to lay down while I call the paramedics." She took hold of him carefully. "Easy now, let me guide you."

Javier frowned with intense anger surging through him. "That bitch shot me. After all that I've done for him, he dared to shoot me. Fuck! This shit is hot!" He winced in pain. "He gon' pay for this." Javier was dizzy. He staggered as Finesse led him to the couch. He laid back. "He shot me, Finesse!" he couldn't help repeating.

Finesse nodded. "I know. Please stop talking so forcefully. Be calm when you speak. We don't want the bullet moving around inside of your abdomen. Oh fuck, fuck, fuck, fuck!" She helped him to lay back on the couch before she got on her phone and called the paramedics. After telling them the extreme extent of the situation, she placed her cellphone on the table and slid beside Javier. "Whatever you do, Javier, do not close your eyes or succumb to the sleepiness that will try to eventually overtake you. You need to keep talking to me. Why would he do this to you? Where do you know him from?"

Javier closed his eyes and opened them wide. "That's my bum ass cousin. I tried to help his li'l dirty ass out more than a few times. I found out that he was stealing from me, so I cut him loose. His broke ass is probably feeling a way about it." Javier closed his eyes. He felt tired and suddenly cold, he thought about the fact that he was screwing Kelis. He wondered if Peto knew. He dismissed the notion that he could have and grew angrier. His eyes rolled to the back of his head.

Finesse tapped his cheek. "No, baby, stay awake. You need to fight right now. Talk to me. What is his name?" Javier was bleeding so bad that the white couch was already drenched with his blood. Finesse worried that if the paramedics didn't get there faster, he would die from the extreme blood loss.

"His name Peto Peralta. He's my paternal aunt's broke-ass son. He's been a hater, but you know how the game goes. It is what it is." Javier licked his lips. "If I die, Mami, make sure you let my pops know that I was about to take over this whole country. Tell him that I didn't need him and that he was a sucka." Javier laughed. "That fool should have been my son, and not the other way around." Javier began to cough. His throat was filled with phlegm and blood.

Finesse rubbed the side of his face. "You can tell him these things yourself because you aren't going anywhere. Now just keep talking. Do you think that he will come back to try and harm you?"

"Mami, if I make it out of this thing alive, I am going to cut his body in half and make sure that he is alive while I am doing it. He's a coward. I didn't even know that he was feeling some type of way towards me. I wouldn't put it past my father to have paid him to take me out." The thought alone made Javier weak. He closed his eyes again, feeling low.

Finesse slapped his cheek. "Wake up baby, please. Keep talking. Why would your father want you dead?"

"He doesn't give a fuck about me. All he cares about is Joaquin and them mafuckas down in La Perla." Javier hated his brother even more now. He wanted his life, Martina's as well. Justina, his baby sister, had always been so warm and welcoming. He didn't know how to feel her about her as of yet, but in his book, both Joaquin and Martina would be killed if he could make it happen and he knew that he could.

19

Finesse was so lost and confused. She didn't know that the Peralta drug empire was as shaky as it was. She was led to believe by her superiors at Quantico that the family was strong and without strife within them. After hearing Javier's rendition of his relationship between himself and Rodolfo, she formed an opinion that told her the family was brutal and unpredictable. *If* what Javier was saying was true and were not illusions of grandeur because of his current physical state, then the family seemed to be in upheaval.

The paramedics made it to the door and began to beat on it. Finesse hollered for them to come in. They rushed inside of the room and got right to work on Javier. Finesse held his hand while they did their thing. Five minutes later, he was placed into the back of their ambulance in serious condition. She grew weary for him. She stayed with him until they got to the hospital. When he fell into a medically induced coma, she finally slipped away. By protocol, she was forced to touch bases with the Federal Bureau of Investigations where she was employed as a Narcotics Agent, unbeknownst to Javier.

***

Emilia stepped up, nudging Joaquin to the side and stepped into Sudan's face. "Look, lady, I don't know who you are or what you think you're running, but you ain't running shit over here. This is La Perla, Puerto Rico. And on this island, I am the queen, Joaquin Peralta is the king. Nobody bows unless they are bowing in prayer. Step off!"

Sudan lowered her eyes; a slightly amused smile came across her gorgeous face. "So, you are Emilia, huh?"

"In the flesh." Emilia mugged her. "Once again, step off. This is a special day for us."

Sudan looked over Emilia's shoulder to stare into the eyes of Joaquin. "Times have changed here in Puerto Rico. Now the woman speaks with balls bigger than the man. It's an honorable day."

Joaquin stepped forward. "Who are you, and why are you here?"

"This land that you know as La Perla has been bought. You are being officially warned to depart from your homes and flee. From one side of the island to the other, all of this land now belongs to my Sudanese people. We will turn it into a beautiful resort and bring back the paradise life. At this moment, it is nothing but filth and litter," she spat, disgusted.

Emilia was back in her face. "Where you see filth, we see the beauty and what we have grown to know as our home. I don't care what you are saying or where you are from, *this* land is our land. And yes, we are ready to die for it." Emilia cocked her gun.

Sudan shook her head. "Such a stupid girl." She grabbed Emilia's neck with blazing speed and placed a blade to her jugular. Sudan's soldiers surrounded them after cocking their assault rifles. She made Emilia get on her knees.

Joaquin upped his .45 and aimed it at Sudan. "What the fuck are you doing?"

"You would never get a bullet off before I murdered this bitch! How can she claim to be a queen when she is so easily subdued? La Perla is full of idiots. Hand over this land or meet your demise in ways that you never thought imaginable. Do it!"

"Fuck this bitch, Joaquin. Shoot her. If she kills me, then I die for La Perla. Shoot her!" Emilia screamed.

Joaquin bit into his bottom lip and got ready to pull the trigger of his gun, but then he imagined Sudan killing Emilia, and his heart grew weary. Although he wasn't the one to normally fold, he couldn't imagine life without Emilia. He lowered the gun. "Alright, please. Take what you want. Just don't hurt my wife. Please."

Sudan sneered at him. "Are you ready to surrender the island?"

"Joaquin, noooo," Emilia begged.

Sudan held the knife firmer against Emilia's jugular until a trickle of blood began to run out of the incision brought forth by the sharpness of the blade. "Shut up girl, you should be wiser. What's it going to be Joaquin?" She began to slice slowly, more blood seeped from Emilia. Sudan held her roughly.

"Alright, alright." He lowered his gun and put his hands in the air. "I surrender the island."

"Fuck." Emilia closed her eyes.

Sudan smiled, looking over at him. She grabbed a handful of Emilia's hair and stuck her face in front of her. "You are lucky that this man loves you. I would have loved to have slaughtered you like a goat." She threw her head forward and kicked her in the back.

Joaquin rushed to Emilia's side. Sudan stood over them. "La Perla, you are no longer the citizens of Puerto Rico. If you wish to stay here on this island, you should know that you will be enslaved by the Sudanese." She mugged Joaquin. "If you or your little idiot crew tries anything unconventional with the exception of fully retreating, you will meet your demise. Trust me." She snickered and gave the signal for her men to follow behind her. A minute later, they stormed away from the scene leaving a cloud of dust in the air.

Emilia jumped up and screamed, "Who was that bitch?! Why did you give up the island to her? Why Joaquin? She just made us look like a bunch of bitches." Emilia had tears running down her cheeks.

Joaquin maintained his composure. "As long as you are alive, everything else will fall into place. Sometimes you have to surrender to conquer. Come on, let's get out of here. There is a lot of work to be done. I won't discuss this right now."

***

Justina waited until Pedro climbed on top of her before she brought her knee upward as hard as she could right into his nut sack. Pedro hollered at the top of his lungs and fell off of her. Justina stood up and picked up her lamp. She ripped it from the wall and brought it down on to Pedro's head at full speed. The lamp shattered and knocked Pedro to the floor. He lay on his stomach groaning in pain. Justina yanked the door of her bedroom open and took off running, bare feet out of it, disbelieving everything that had taken place. She couldn't fathom why Pedro would want to kill Martina, and then force himself upon her. She felt sick and terrified. As she was running out of the shack, Joaquin and Emilia were pulling up to it. She diverted her escape and ran full speed into Joaquin's arms. "He killed mama! He killed her and tried to rape me. He took her life, Joaquin. I can't believe he..." Justina's eyes crossed before she fainted.

Joaquin laid her on the ground. "Justina! Justina! What's going on?"

Emilia caught Pedro sneaking out of their shack with the bloody knife in his hand. "Hey!" she hollered.

"Aw shit." Pedro saw that he had been spotted, he took off running.

Emilia was in hot pursuit. "Hey!" She ran as fast as she could, kicking off her wedges. She was thankful that Pedro was heavy set and out of shape. She closed the distance between them almost immediately. When she got behind him, she upped her .380 and pulled the trigger twice.

Boom! Boom!

Pedro flipped around and fell dizzily onto a bunch of silver garbage cans. The bullets burned holes within his back, ripping through various muscles and tendons. He groaned in pain and forced himself to stand up. He swiped the knife at Emilia. "What did you do? Huh, what did you do?" Emilia hollered. She frowned and finished him before she could change her mind or Joaquin could stop her. She popped him six times facially, then stood over his smoking body with hot gun shells all around it on the ground.

Joaquin caught up to her breathing hard. He saw the state of Pedro and exhaled loudly. "Damn," he shook his head, "Come on baby. We gotta get Justina up. I need to know what she's saying this Cabron has done."

"Yeah, let's do that." She mugged Pedro's corpse one final time before she turned her backs on him and jogged to Justina who was still passed out in the back of Joaquin's truck.

Chapter 3

Joaquin grabbed the big shovel that was full of muddy, wet dirt and tossed the thick contents of it into the grave of Martina. Tears rolled down his cheeks along with the drizzle of the rain that fell from the sky over the cemetery. He pushed his dark shades back up on his nose and felt weak in the knees. He still couldn't believe that Pedro had taken Martina's life. He should have killed him when he had the chance. He felt guilty and naive.

Emilia came and stood beside him. She wrapped her left arm around his waist, while she looked into Martina's grave. Her bottom lip quivered. "I knew I should have killed him when he first came back from the States. We should have never allowed for that rat to keep any air in his lungs. Now, look at what Pedro has done. Not only has he taken way a great woman, but Justina will never be the same. I curse the day we ever gave him a second chance." Emilia crossed herself with the sign of the crucifix.

Joaquin dropped the shovel and looked down at his mother's coffin as rain popped off of it and the mud that was now atop it. "My mother was dying of cervical cancer. The doctors had given her less than six months to live. I can only imagine the physical pain that she was going through daily. I wish I could have been there for her more than I was. I hate this."

Emilia scoffed, "If they gave her six months to live, then that meant that she had six months to live, approximately. That bitch ass Pedro took her six months too soon. It's not fair. The world is just not fair. Never will we allow for second chances again. Now, we are both motherless. What a world?"

Joaquin pulled her closer to him. "I know, but what are we going to do? We can only play the cards that we are dealt." He kissed the side of Emilia's forehead.

Emilia closed her eyes briefly. When she opened them, they were watery. "She called me her daughter and her baby. I always felt so very loved by her. She was perfect. Martina was the heart and soul of La Perla. Now that both she and my mother are gone, I don't want to be here any longer, Joaquin. I hate this island now, especially with the Sudanese rolling around in Hummers like they own the place. I think it's time that we leave." She turned to face him. The rain started to come down harder.

"Leave Emilia? But where will we go? All we know is La Perla. All we know is Puerto Rico."

Emilia shook her head. "Not anymore, we don't. I don't feel that there is anything left for us here. We have to go." She looked into the grave one more time and covered her face. "We have to, and you know it. There is nothing left in La Perla for us but death and devastation. I can't take the pain of being here any longer. It hurts too bad." She walked away crying tears of defeat and longing.

Justina watched from afar. She waited until Emilia jogged to Joaquin's truck and slammed the door before she walked up to Joaquin, sliding her hand into his. She kissed his cheek and laid her head on his shoulder. "I miss her already, Joaquin. What will we ever do without our precious mother?"

Joaquin exhaled and allowed for the tears to drop off of his chin. "We have to stay strong and keep on moving. Mama was a fighter. She believed that struggle and sacrifice made a person strong and grateful. She taught us that adversity builds character. She will always live in our hearts; no death could ever take her away from us."

Justina was quiet for a moment. "I think Emilia's is right. We need to get up out of La Perla, there is nothing here for us any longer. We don't stand a chance on this disease-infested island. I think we should leave as soon as possible."

"Leave where? Where will we go, Justina? All we know is La Perla." Even the thought of leaving behind his island and all of his friends felt like a stake was being driven into Joaquin's heavy heart.

"That's where daddy comes in at. He says that we could come to Miami with him. He says that over there we could live good. It's safer, cleaner, and there we could all get a fresh start." She stepped in front of him. "Sooner or later you are going to get Emilia pregnant. Do you wish for your child to be born in a dump like La Perla, or a place like Miami where it is always beautiful, and your children will at least have a fighting chance at normalcy? After a while, you have to start thinking about the future instead of the here and now. Remaining in La Perla is selfish and reckless. Only a fool would continue to succumb to these conditions even though they had a way out." It began to rain harder, so Justina pulled her hood taut over her head. "I know that you make your own decisions, Joaquin and that you are obsessed with this island. If you really care about Emilia like you say you do, you will get her off of it. If you don't, she will be dead in a matter of months. Believe that." Justina kissed his cheek. "I'll be in the truck." She walked to the tip of Martina's grave said a quick prayer just as lightning flashed through the air. She kissed her hand when she finished and blew the invisible kiss to her mother before she jogged away and back to the truck where Emilia sat crying her eyes out.

Joaquin fell to his knees as soon as she departed. The thunder roared over his head. The wind picked up speed and caused the rain to thrash about violently. He allowed his tears to fall freely. "I miss you, mama. I don't know how I let this dude snake us like this, but I know it's all my fault. I can't seem to cope right now. All I do is think about you and where I went wrong. Please forgive me, mama. I swear I didn't think he would clap back like this. Forgive me and I promise to never slip up like this again." He lowered his forehead to the dirt. "Damn, this shit is killing me!" he hollered. He fell back on his haunches and tilted his head toward the sky. His face was repeatedly splashed with rain for the next thirty minutes while he prayed. After he finished up his chat with God, he hopped up. "I gotta get my people off the island and to safety," he said this in defeat as Emilia had. "Once they're safe, I'm coming back for La Perla, my homeland, by any and every means. I promise you that mama."

He growled through clenched teeth, "You have raised a king that will never let your death be in vain." He lowered his forehead to the mud and cried until his heart couldn't take anymore. He stood up strong and determined.

***

Javier looked himself over in the full-length mirror and ran his hand over the gauze that was attached to his stomach and shoulder. He smiled at the sight of them. He was heavily muscled with tattoos all over him. He had a bit of a gut from drinking a lot of Robitussin and Lean, but he still admired what he saw from his reflection. "Damn, I got shot two weeks ago and I'm back up and at 'em like a champion. Mafuckas can't hold me down." He side-stepped and tooted a gram of Sinaloa heroin up each nostril from the top of his dresser. He pinched his nose and tilted his head back. "Damn, this shit is strong." His eyes watered.

Finesse eased into the room wearing a pair of small boy shorts and a white beater with no bra. She slipped her arms around his waist. "Now, you heard what the doctors said. They said you should be on bed rest. The only reason they discharged you is because of this whole COVID epidemic. The hospital beds are at capacity and they can't afford the space. That doesn't mean that you can't have some serious things going on inside of you, Javier."

Javier waved her off. His eyelids began to droop. "Man, I'm good. Nigga caught me slipping. Okay, so what? Shit happens. The bullets ain't do no damage. What am I supposed to do, sit back and cry about being popped twice? Yeah right. I gotta get back to the money. Mafuckas calling for orders in Atlanta, Savannah, and all over Florida. I gotta fulfill them if I wanna eat. Me laying in a hospital bed don't show shit but a major sign of weakness."

Finesse rolled her eyes. "You sound like dumb ass Trump and the whole not wearing a mask thing." She sighed. "Once again, Javier, resting and getting back to full health doesn't make you weak. It makes you smart. You need to give your body time to recuperate. You lost a lot of blood, and that can be catastrophic for anybody, especially internally."

"Yeah, well, I ain't anybody. I'm Javier Peralta, head of the Peralta Cartel. Fuck everybody else and how they recover, that shit ain't got nothing to do with me. Long as I got my drank and this dope, I'm good to go like the FDA stamped and approved me." He laughed at his own joke.

Finesse didn't find him amusing. "Okay, so what's your plan?" She started to get dressed.

"I just told you. I got a bunch of drop-offs to make sure happens, then I gotta collect my cash, and from there I gotta make my presence known in the gutters of Miami. My team already setting up all over the Grove. So far there is little resistance by a few niggaz that need to be smashed, but we handling them, and the money is coming in already. Next is the South Beach takeover, then the strip, and then Opa-Locka. The money is crazy out there, we gotta expand. We gotta up our weaponry though cause them clowns out that way are playing for keeps."

Finesse nodded her head. "It sounds like you're about to be busy. I guess I'll leave you to it." She looked him over in disappointment and walked out of the room. She disliked the fact that he was being so defiant. He didn't take the fact that he had nearly been killed seriously, and to her that was ridiculous. She was ready to end their closeness and the bond that they had begun to build. She figured she would strictly stick to the script that the FBI had her assigned to. That seemed to be smarter for her anyway, she decided.

Javier waited until she reached the living room before he slipped behind her and wrapped his arms around her body startling her. She tensed. He laughed and kissed her on the back of the neck. "I can tell that something ain't right with you, Mami. What is it?"

Finesse slipped from his arms. "You mean other than the fact that you're acting like a self-centered, unaware, asshole that is ungrateful for his being alive? Huh, let's see. I don't know." She crossed her arms.

Javier mugged her. "Damn, why the fuck you acting all stank and shit? Just cause I wanna get back to the money, are you kidding me?"

"Javier, I don't care what you do, quite honestly. But do you understand that you could have been killed? Do you also understand that to save us, I had to kill a man and that I still have to answer for his death in court? It's been kept hush-hush for the most part, but in the wake of this new movement pushing for change when it comes to minorities being gunned down in the street, prosecutors could easily flip on me down the road just to appease the public."

"Never. This is Miami, Florida. We have the 'Stand Your Ground Law'. That muthafucka was in here popping me up and you finished him. Luckily, I had my cameras rolling. The cameras caught his ass before, during, and after the whole thing, or shit would've probably been a lot different."

"Yeah and all of those things you should be happy and thankful to God for," she reminded him.

Javier laughed. "I am God. What, you want me to be thankful to myself?" He busted up laughing. He could feel the pain from his life-saving surgery inside of his gut. He stepped into the kitchen and opened the refrigerator. "Nah, I am thankful, Mami. I just got a funny way of showing it." He grabbed the orange juice out of it and twisted off the cap. He leaned against the stove; he could also feel the heroin making him lazy. He began to slowly nod out.

Finesse stepped in front of him. "Javier, I'ma be gone for a few weeks. I have business to take care of. I'll be in touch with you. All I ask is that you be careful, be smart, and take it easy." She kissed his lips.

"Aw bitch, by the time you come back, I would have been made a few million. I gotta kill up some shit first, but then it's on," he slurred. His eyes closed before he dropped the orange juice bottle to the floor, nodding off of the Sinaloa.

"Yeah, well you heard what I said." She shook her head at him and left the kitchen. She'd already tapped his phones and left multiple bugs all over his home as directed by her superiors. While, at first, she felt guilty about setting him up and doing what they'd requested, now she was feeling that it was warranted due to Javier's cockiness and utter disregard for anybody outside of himself.

"I'm 'bout to get money, Finesse. I'm finna shut Miami down! The three-oh-five belongs to the Peralta Cartel. Know that!" he hollered. He slid down the refrigerator with his eyes closed, and his ass in the puddle of juice. He didn't care, there was nothing more important at that time than his nodding. "Get money bitch! You'll be back!"

Chapter 4

Two months later...

"Joaquin, I still cannot believe that you could be so stubborn. Instead of you staying right off of South Beach with me and Papi, you choose to allow for him to buy out ten apartments here in this God-forsaken project complex. Did you stop for a second to think about how this will affect Emilia down the road?" Justina said this while she looked out of Joaquin's Lincoln Navigator truck completely dismayed.

"Justina, the fact that I was willing to leave La Perla should be enough victory for both you and Rodolfo. I already feel sick to my stomach and as if I've betrayed my people. I don't need your continuous nagging. It only adds to the frustration I feel deep inside of my heart, and when it comes to Emilia, I have her best interest in mind at all times." He looked out of the window and mugged the Cordoba Courts housing projects that were located inside of the deadly slums of Miami Gardens. "Besides, as a man, I desire to start from the bottom and work my way to the top. I don't need to stay in some mansion with a father that abandoned us for this life. I will figure things out, I always do."

Justina eyed him and took a deep breath, slowly blowing it out. "There is so much of the stubborn part of our mother inside of you that it's scary. What can I say? You are my big brother, and I love you with all that I am. If you need me, you know where to find me." She leaned over and kissed his cheek, before hugging his neck.

"I love you too, Justina. Just trust me. I know what I have to accomplish, and I will not fail Emilia." He hugged her tightly.

"I trust you." She grabbed her Gucci purse from the console of the truck and opened the door. "Be safe out here, Joaquin. This isn't La Perla, this is Miami, Florida. There is no reason for struggle or strife here." She blew him a kiss and got into the waiting limousine that Rodolfo had sent for her. It pulled off and left Joaquin in deep thought.

As soon as Justina pulled away, Emilia opened the passenger's door and sat in the seat there. She looked over at Joaquin concerned. "Okay Papi, we're here. We have thirty of our people from La Perla with us. How are we going to feed them, and what are your plans? Do you think it was a bright idea to bring half of La Perla here?" she said this last part with a hint of sarcasm, but the slug landed inside Joaquin's heart.

Joaquin grabbed her by the neck and kissed her lips. He licked all over them and slid his tongue into her mouth. Emilia moaned and fell into him. Joaquin rushed the front of her jeans until he felt the heat radiating from between her thighs. Her pussy lips pressed against the jean material. She could feel her nipples spike. Joaquin broke the kiss; she fell away breathing hot and bothered.

Emilia licked her lips and tried to get control of her breathing. "What was that all about?"

Joaquin mugged the structure of the project buildings again. "Emilia, I need for you to know that I got you and that I love you with all of my heart. I understand that you could have had a great life in the Bronx with the other man, but I promise you to give you more than what he is rendering to Cecilia because you deserve it."

"Joaquin, I don't want some other life in the Bronx. I want and need you. All I need in this world is you. We left La Perla as a team, and we arrived here in Miami as a team. I will follow you. That is my place. I will follow you to the ends of the earth because that's what real love does." She leaned across the console and took a hold of the back of his neck. "Besides, when I see this project building, I see us conquering it and this entire area. I see us turning this new land into La Perla, and I see us slowly spreading our people throughout Miami. We deserve to be free. We deserve to be wealthy. With you at the helms, Joaquin, I know that we will get there. Baby, I believe in you and I am with you through it all. Let's make it happen." She searched his eyes for a moment, then she was kissing his lips all over again, lustfully and hungrily.

Joaquin broke the kiss and rubbed the sides of her face. He looked her over with life infatuation and possessiveness. "I swear to God, I love you, Emilia. You give me the strength that only a man's better half could render unto him. It is because of you and the strong backbone that you give me that I will be able to do what I am about to do with this land." He kissed her forehead and smiled.

***

That night, Joaquin filled the remaining nine apartments with the families and the members of his close-knit troops from La Perla. He promised them that for as long as they lived in the apartments that they would never have to worry about the rent or the utilities. He provided them with groceries and weapons for their security. When he finished with all of this, he called a meeting for his troops on the floor that his father had completely rented out for his use. They met up in one of the empty apartments that had yet to be rented, but the door was found to be opened. The troops from La Perla lined up thirty deep and stood in formation as Joaquin stepped in front of them with Emilia sitting in a chair on his right side. He looked them all over and stopped abruptly. He was shirtless and jacked with muscles all over his body.

"The first thing I need for you guys to know is that the reason you are here right now is because I personally picked you to be. There is a war going on inside of La Perla that we at this moment are not strong enough to meet head-on. Now, ignorance would have forced me to push forward anyway. If I would have done so, I am sure that we would have suffered many casualties. Many of our people would have been lost and the result would have been the Sudanese taking over our land in blood anyway. I could not, as your leader, go that route. Instead, I have chosen for us to bring La Perla right here to Miami. We will move forward with all of our plans to build up our homeland and to get into a position where we will be strong enough to conquer it as we should be. For us to meet the requirements that it will take, we must acquire enough funds. Money equals power. With money, we can build up our arsenal and our connections. If we can accrue some major support from a few of the other Latin bosses from the surrounding islands, we will not only be able to go at the Sudanese the way we need to to reestablish our homeland, but we will be able to go at and annihilate them."

Jimenez, a young cold-hearted shooter born and raised in San Juan, raised his hand and Joaquin pointed to him. He was five feet and seven inches tall, slim, with brown eyes, thick eyebrows, and curly hair. "The way all of this looks is as if we are all cowards. We allowed for a bunch of Africans to run us away from our land, and now we are here trying to pick up the broken pieces of our manhood. I feel like a coward. I would have rather died on Puerto Rican land than to have come here."

Emilia mugged him. "Then why did you come?"

He turned to her. "Because the Sudanese have already burned down my shack and all of those on my row. I didn't have anything to return to, and my mother begged me to help her to have a new beginning. That is why I am here, much like so many others in this room. By circumstance."

Emilia stood up. "Then are you saying that you are a part of us, or apart from us? Which is it?" Now the entire room was looking at Jimenez.

He balled his fist and tapped it over his heart. I am Puerto Rican, and the only family that I have is the family in this room. Do not mistake my words for those of being against you because that is not accurate. I am here, and I am loyal to Joaquin as our leader. So far, he hasn't steered us wrong. I was only speaking my mind."

Emilia stepped into his face and looked into his eyes. Hers were menacing. "Well, you've spoken your peace. We've all heard it. With that being said, what is your next move? Are you still ready to die for every member in this room right here, or are you double-minded? Tell me, we all want to know."

Jimenez held his head high. "I have one mind and it remains loyal to our cause, and the people in this room. That's where I am, and that's where I will remain." He took a step back in line and nodded his head at Joaquin.

Joaquin nodded back at him. Emilia stared at him for a moment longer, and then she went and took her seat. Joaquin walked up to Jimenez and placed his hand on his shoulder. "I promise you, my brother, that we will recover our land. It belongs to us. We will use America as a land to get rich, and when we become superior, we will conquer what rightfully belongs to us. You have my word on this. Please be patient. That goes for all of you. Patience and intelligence will go hand in hand. We are to become royal. Our families deserve the best lives that we can possibly give to them. We must fight to overcome our adversities and to defeat our adversaries. We are one family, and one clan. Now, who's with me?"

The entire room began to hug and cheer with each other. Joaquin walked up to and hugged each member in the room. He promised them that brighter days were coming. He promised them that very soon they would be seeing more money than they ever had in their entire lives. He painted a picture that made it hard for each person present to not bite off into. Joaquin was determined and driven to stand on his word as a man and leader.

***

The next morning, he sat down and had a two-hour meeting with Rodolfo as a business partner and not as a son, though Rodolfo found it hard to split the difference. Joaquin had three-hundred thousand dollars left to his name after he helped so many of his people make it over to Florida from Puerto Rico. He slid the remaining money across his kitchen table to Rodolfo. "Inside is three-hundred thousand dollars of my hard-earned money. Take it and give me as much coke, heroin, and weapons as you can. Do not give me anything extra, only give to me what I am paying for. Can you do this, or must I go and find another plug?"

Rodolfo picked up the dirty money and flicked through the big bills. He smiled at Joaquin. "You haven't been in America for more than forty-eight hours and already you are looking to jump into the game. Are you sure you would not like to learn about the city first?"

"Guns will help me to navigate. Murder will help others to understand that I am here, that La Perla is here. The money will help me to bring over more of my people. Time is something that I do not have. Give me the things that I desire, or I will be forced to find another avenue." Emilia came and stood behind Joaquin with a scowl on her pretty face. She placed both of her hands on his shoulders.

Rodolfo nodded and stood up. "By six o'clock tonight, you will have everything that you need to get started." He paused. "Joaquin, I know that you and I haven't had the strongest relationship, but you should know that I love you and I am here for you. Whatever you have in mind, you don't have to do. I am more than capable of providing for both you and your wife."

Joaquin stood up. "Any man that leans on his parents to provide for him and his family is a bitch!"

Emilia frowned. "We don't believe in handouts. We will hustle from the mud up. We could never accept one cent from you, or anybody else for that matter. Joaquin is more than capable."

Joaquin lowered his eyes. "In six months, I will be in a position to assist you. Never offer to weaken me as a man. Your sole position is to make sure that I get everything on my own. That is the definition of a man."

Rodolfo held up his hands in surrender and fascination. He smiled. "Duly noted." He only wished that Javier could have been so headstrong. "I apologize. It's like I said, you will have everything that you need by six o'clock tonight. That is my word." With that said, he left feeling prouder than he had ever felt in his life.

Emilia locked the door and walked up to Joaquin. "Nobody knows you but me. I understand your heart and your mind. We are one."

Joaquin's eyes were pinned on the front door that his father had stepped out of. "Very soon this city will belong to us. Mark my words. Miami will be the new La Perla."

Hood Rich

Chapter 5

Javier stepped out of cherry red Bentley truck and dusted the remnants of the exotic strand of weed off of his lap. He took four hard pulls from the big Cuban cigar stuffed with the strand and flicked the quarter blunt into the street carelessly. He pushed the Chanel glasses back on his nose and jacked his gold Gucci belt that offset his Yves St. Laurent fit. He was matching designer clothing, flexing hard with a neck full of jewelry and diamonds that glistened in the South Beach moonlight. He stepped away from his truck with four shooters behind him that were assigned to his Peralta Cartel as hittas. The valet hopped into his truck and rolled away. Javier was rolling off of four Percocets and a gram of Sinaloa heroin. His eyes were low, and the exotic weed had only added to his high. He smacked his lips and stepped on to the red carpet of Nobu. The paparazzi flashed their cameras with click after click, and while he knew they were shooting to capture the many celebrities that were going in and out of the club, his ego told him that they were also there to snap him. Unbeknownst to Javier, more than a few of the shot takers worked for the FBI.

Javier stepped up to the bouncer and squeezed his eyelids closed. His mouth was drier than a sixty-year old's pussy. He wiped his lips and squinted at the big, Cuban, baldheaded bouncer. "Say, Chico, my name is Javier and I got four of my homeboys wit' me, reserved for VIP. Look it up." He staggered and started to scratch his chest and arms. The Percocets always made him itch as if he had fleas. It was one of the only things he hated about the pills.

The bouncer scrolled down at his small tablet until he found his name. Besides his name, it said that he had only reserved for two of his homeboys to roll through with him. "We got a problem Pa Pa. Two of your boys can't come in. I mean unless they are on the list their own, right." He showed him the tablet.

Javier opened his eyes as wide as he could. He stared at the screen. "Nah Poppa, that's impossible. I'm Javier Peralta. Don't no mafucka put a limit on what I can do."

The bouncer was unimpressed. "Yeah, well that may be true in other places, but here at Nobu, you are only as important as your reservation. Your reservation says that you can only bring two guests along with you. If you wanna challenge that, you can leave and call the manager. If not, you can cut two of them loose and have them meet up with you later. It's as simple as that."

Javier mugged him. He laughed. "Say Pa, you take this job so serious that you'd be willing to screw around with somebody like me, huh? You fuckin' tell me that I can't bring two of my team members with me and you think this is okay, huh?"

The bouncer curled his lip. "What you gon' do man? You're holding up my line."

Javier looked both ways, and then behind him. Four white couples were waiting to check themselves in with the bouncer so they could go and enjoy a nice meal. This only infuriated Javier. Javier pulled out a knot of hundreds totaling twenty thousand dollars. "How much is it going to take, huh? One hundred, two hundred, a stack?" He peeled off ten one-hundred-dollar bills.

The bouncer tried to play coy. He looked over Javier's shoulder. "I usually ain't supposed to take money from guests, but if that shit wound up in my suit jacket pocket, then I mean it is what it is."

Javier stared at him for a long time. Then after concluding that he would make the bouncer pay for his transgressions at a later time, he pulled the suit coat's pocket to him and stuffed the thousand dollars inside of it feeling like he was being punked. "Alright nigga, let us through now."

"Enjoy your night, gentleman." The bouncer unhooked the velvet rope and stepped aside.

Javier's entire team mugged him as they walked past him and into the restaurant-styled nightclub. The dance floor was already packed. There was loud music blaring Pit Bull, the women were shaking and dancing provocatively in time to the music. Javier smiled. There were two stages with strippers on them getting down. He watched them for a second with a smile on his face, then he moved further inside. Above and directly across from the stages were the VIP sections. Before they could make it fully into the dancing crowd, a bottle girl walked up to him. She was light-skinned with brown eyes, smooth skin, and a body of a goddess. Javier found himself salivating at the mouth.

"Good evening, fellas. Are you VIP customers or are you looking for a normal night out here at Nobu?"

"I don't do shit that ain't first class. We're important all the way. Now, direct me to my section," he ordered, looking her up and down.

"Before I do that, I'ma need yo name to make sure you posed to be over there. Can you run it to me, mane?" she asked, looking up at Javier and disliking his rude demeanor. She pulled out an identical-looking tablet to the one that the bouncer was using.

"Javier Peralta. Party of four. It might say two on there, but we just straighten that shit out wit' homeboy at the door."

She scrolled down until she found his name. The bouncer had already made the correction and added two to their party. "Seems to me that everything is fine. If you could kindly follow me, I'll take you to your section. Y'all want me to send any special girls up there or anything? We have quite a nice selection here, guaranteed you'll like what you get."

Javier watched her ass jiggled inside of the small shorts. The cheeks were hanging out of the material. He imagined smacking that ass and shivered. "Say Shawty, what yo name is?"

"Amanda, and I'll be your bottle girl for the night." She looked over her shoulder at him.

Javier smiled and gazed back down to her ass. "Yeah, you can send some of your choice women up here for my home-boys, but I personally wanna fuck wit' you. I don't care what that bill gon' look like either." He pulled nineteen thousand out and waved it in her face. Javier felt like he knew how most women operated in Miami. They didn't understand talk, they only understood the sight of money. Money opened doors, being broke got those doors closed in your face. He wanted every bad bitch to know that he was having that major life-changing money.

Amanda led them into their section and directed for Javier's shooters to get comfortable. Javier stepped into her face and smiled showing off his mouth full of gold. Amanda blushed. "I sho' wish I could spend some time with you. You kinda remind me of a finer version of Shemar Moore, and I grew up liking him. Only thang bout that is that they don't allow me to spend too much time in one section. I gotta keep it moving. Dats what my papers say too." Her southern accent was strong, and Javier loved it.

"Where you from, baby girl?" He needed to know where they made such sexy black women like her. Once he found out, he was sure he would be taking a trip out that way.

"I'm from Nawlins', baby, born and bred. That's the Creole cockpit right there," she said this proudly.

Javier stepped into her face. "Shawty you quit."

44

She frowned at him. "What?"

"I said you quit; you don't work here no more. I want you to come and work for me." He leaned further into her face. He could see the glitter sprayed across her perfect nose and cheeks.

"I ain't been working here but three weeks. I can't quit. My house note runs me every bit of twelve hundred a month. I got so many other bills that even thanking bout 'em make me stressed out, so I'm sorry, you fine and all dat shit thurr, but I can't quit my gig." She got ready to walk away.

Javier grabbed her arm. "You quit this mafucka and come work for me, I'll give you a ten-thousand-dollar signing bonus right now." He licked his thumb and began to count through the blue faces.

Amanda's eyes got big. "You serious?"

"As a heart attack. Come fuck wit' me, tonight." He looked her up and down. She was so thick down low, and small up top. She was slightly bow-legged, and he could tell that she was younger than him. He had to have her.

Amanda looked over her shoulder. "How 'bout you give me a moment to go up here and leave dis job behind. But fore I do dat, what you gon' have me doing working for you? What's the name of yo company?"

"The Peralta Cartel, and you gon' be my personal assistant. That's all you gotta know. Now go handle yo bidness and bring yo ass back. Time is muthafuckin' money." He smacked her ass and squeezed her booty.

"Okay, I'll be right back." She made haste out of the section.

Javier nodded his head. She had to be out of her mind if she thought that he would ever give her ten thousand dollars for anything. All he wanted to do was hit the pussy. If it was good, then he'd consider paying a few of her bills, but the total would never come anywhere near ten thousand dollars. He was sure of that. He was about to turn around and sit on the red leather couch when a dark-skinned man with long dreadlocks and gray eyes stepped to the door of his section. Javier's men jumped up and came up behind him. "Nigga, can I help you?" Javier asked coldly.

Mudman stared into Javier's eyes without breaking the contact. "Say, Mane, I was over there minding my bidness when I looked over here and saw you wit' yo paws on one of the shawties from the hood. You care to tell me why you did?" Mudman's country accent was twice as strong as Amanda's.

"What? Man, we don't give no fucks about what you saw. Don't worry about it, mufucka! Do you know who I am?" Javier snapped.

Mudman shook his head. "Nope, and I don't give a fuck either. A better question for you to ask and have answered is who the fuck is Mudman. That's the question."

Javier scanned the club and saw that it didn't appear that Mudman had anybody with him. Javier knew that there was strength in numbers. He grew confident. "My name is Javier Peralta. I am King of the Peralta Cartel, and if I was you, I would keep it moving before this turn into something as ugly as your face."

Mudman lowered his eyes and flexed his fingers. "It's nice to meet you, Javier. They call me Mudman, and I am a muthafuckin' Cartel Killa. I don't give a fuck about you or those bitch ass niggaz behind you. If you knew what was good for you, y'all would stay away from our Louisiana hoes. This yo last warning."

Amanda came back and strolled into the VIP section. "Okay, I'm ready to go." She looked Javier over and, for the first time, paid attention to who he was glaring at. She cursed under her breath. "Fuck! Mudman, what's going on?"

Mudman shook his head. "Nothin', y'all enjoy your-selves." He began to walk away.

Javier's troops were about to go at him when Javier stopped them. "No, let him go. Clearly, he was drunk." He mugged Mudman as he made his way through the crowd with a black hoodie over his head. As he passed, people got out of his way. "Who is that dude, Amanda?"

Amanda sighed. "That's my cousin. He just moved to Miami from Baton Rouge. He brought a bunch of his low-down dirty savages with him because they got into some trouble back out that way, but he's harmless. Don't pay him any mind. Come on, let's go." She wrapped her arm into his and pulled him out of the section.

Javier followed reluctantly with Mudman's chilling words playing over and over in his head. *What did he mean that he was a Cartel killa? Was it a threat? The truth?* Javier seriously wondered.

Hood Rich

Chapter 6

"I'on know where you from, Lil' daddy, but down dare in Nawlins, we get it in," Amanda said this as she stepped into the bedroom in an all-white bodysuit that clung to her curves so much so that it looked as if it had been painted on to her. She stopped at the foot of the bed and popped back on her legs.

Javier picked his face up from the potent plate of Sinaloa. He pinched his nostrils for a moment and tilted his head back as the raw began to drip down the back of his throat, and the strong feeling of heaviness came upon him. He stood up with his eyes closed. He opened them, looking Amanda up and down. "Damn, Mamita. I knew you were strapped, but I ain't know you was holding like that."

Amanda came around the bed and stood just to the left of him. "You been running dat dare mouth dis whole time, and back when we were at da club, it's time fa you to let me see if you can stand up to all dat shit dat you been saying." She looked into his eyes. "Well, what you gotta say bout dat?" She slowly turned around in a slow circle. When Javier was able to see how far her ass poked out, he cursed out loud. She laughed. "Dis dat Louisiana right here, daddy."

Javier wiped his nose and frowned. He ran his tongue over his teeth and tried his best to avoid nodding. He grabbed her. Amanda shrieked before she crashed into his chest. Javier took hold of her juicy ass and squeezed the cheeks. "Bitch, you think just cause you all thick like this that you runnin' shit'?" he asked, his words slightly slurring.

Amanda looked into his eyes. "You muthafuckin' right. You betta respect what's presented in front of you. I ain't seen nan one of those Miami girls built like dis. I know fa sho' that I'm a high commodity." She smiled and rubbed his shoulders.

Javier smacked his lips. "Bitch, what? Man, you gotta be kidding me. First of all, it doesn't matter how much ass you got back there, you still black. It's all kinds of Spanish bitches walking around the three-oh-five that's murdering you. Don't get shit twisted. Second to that, you dealing wit' a boss. That means that you are especially lucky to be in my presence. Now, I'm finna hit this pussy and I might let you sleep in the guest room afterward. You gotta problem wit' that?"

Amanda lowered her eyes and pushed him away from her. "Fuck you mean, I'm black? What dat got to do wit' anythang? Don't tell me you thank yo bitches better than me and my sistas? If that's the case den, we got a muthafuckin' problem."

Javier was still looking at the place on his chest where she had pushed him. He slowly trailed his eyes up to meet hers. "Bitch, did you just put yo' hands on a boss?"

Amanda waved him off. "Mane, ain't nobody got time for this shit here. I'm 'bout to call myself an Uber. It's clear dat you outta yo' fuckin' mind, dats what dat is right there." She walked out of the master bedroom, and into the guestroom where she'd discarded her clothes. She sat on the bed and began to kick off her high heels.

Javier appeared at the doorway with an evil sneer on his face. "Aw, so now yo' li'l punk-ass getting sensitive?"

"Who da fuck is you talking too like dat? I don't know how dese other girls letting you flex on dem, but dis ain't dat, Playboy. You gon have to respect me or get yo' ass checked. I'm from Nawlins and we got heart, fuck you thought dis here was."

Javier stepped into the room and closed the door. "You just mad 'cause I told the truth. Bitch, you know mafuckin' well dat you black hoes can't fuck wit Latinas. You walking around dis mafucka wit yo' head too far in the clouds. I had to bring you back to earth, and now that you back you finna what you came here for. That's what's good."

Amanda mugged him. She stood up and walked closer to Javier. "First of all, the most beautiful, the strongest, and the most powerful woman on earth is both the black and brown woman. I'm not gon' allow a chauvinistic pig like you to divide us when we are all in this struggle together. Secondly, you are Puerto Rican, dumb ass nigga. You got a large portion of black in you, whether you know it or not. Thirdly, I ain't gotta do shit that I don't wanna do. If you thank you gon' make me do anythang den we bout to see bout dat. I grew up with four brothers. I was the baby, and they all tried me for one reason or another. Shit wasn't sweet wit' dem, and it ain't gon be sweet wit yo ass. So, wit' dat being said, what you talkin' 'bout?"

Javier laughed. He closed his eyes for a second and nodded briefly. He opened them back and mugged her. "So, you saying I done brought you all the way to this mansion for you to say you ain't fuckin'?"

Amanda glared at him. "If you thank dat I'd ever let a low-life mafucka like you get tween' dese here thighs after hearing yo dumb ass rhetoric, you got the game fucked up. 'Specially dis here, player. You can't even kiss my ass if I sat on fire." She snickered and turned her back to him. "Bout to call me an Uber and get the fuck out of dis mansion." She turned around. "And for the record, the only reason I came here is 'cause you said you was gon' give me ten-thousand dollars. To be honest, I was feeling one of yo potnas' more den I was you. You're too short for me."

That did it. Javier closed the distance between them quickly. He took a hold of her neck and picked her up in the air with extreme strength. He carried her to the bed and slammed her on it. Once she was on her back, he hopped on top of her and took the handcuffs out of his pocket. He cuffed her left wrist to the metal headboard. Her right one punched him in the jaw. He slapped her and then cuffed that wrist beside the first bound one. Once it was bound, she began to kick wildly at him. Javier eased backward and stood at the end of the bed fully undressing himself.

"Say Mane, what the fuck dis bout right here? You better let me go. Let me out of these handcuffs. What da fuck is wrong wit' you, homeboy?" Amanda shouted.

Javier opened the top drawer of his dresser and pulled out a .45. He cocked it and aimed it at Amanda. "Mami, you making way too much noise right now. Shut yo muthafuckin' mouth."

Amanda closed her lips briefly. "I just wanna know what's going on? I don't want no problems wit' you."

Javier shook his head. "It's too late for that shit. Bitch, you was talking that tough Tony garbage. Why are you nutting up all of a sudden?"

Amanda swallowed her spit. "I thought we were just talking shit to one another. Why did you get all serious?" She pulled at her binds to no relief.

Javier climbed on the bed. He sat the gun on the night table on his side of the bed. He turned back to Amanda and sized up her body. "On some real shit, Mamita, I ain't never seen a woman this perfectly thick before. I mean, you got the thighs." He rubbed all over them squeezing as he spoke. "You got the ass, and I can only imagine what between them looks like." He got on his knees and spread her legs and climbed in between them. He lowered his face to her crotch and sniffed the fabric at the same time he pushed the cloth into her gap and caused her to have a camel toe. He licked up and down her covered groove. "Damn bitch, you so thick." He pushed her legs further apart.

Amanda laid back and placed her feet on the blankets. She looked down at him, praying that he wasn't some kind of maniac. She was wishing that she had let somebody know where she was headed. She made a mental note that if she was allowed to come from under this situation with her life that from there on out, she would never leave the club with a man that she'd just met. Secondly, she would always send pics of any foreign destination when she arrived at it. *Oh, hindsight was twenty-twenty,* she thought.

Javier rubbed her pussy through the material until it was leaking right through the crotch. Her lips became visible. He shivered and sucked them through the panties causing her to moan loudly. He licked up and down her groove for five minutes. Amanda's thighs were wide open. He took a hold of the panties and yanked them roughly from her frame. The discarded material was then flung to the floor. Her pussy appeared before him freshly shaven, engorged, and leaking. It was so fat that the sight of it caused him to groan. He played with the thick lips. "Damn bitch, all you had to do was show me this mafucka in the club and I would've given you ten G's on the strength." He continued to rub it before he opened her up and slid his tongue as deep into her as it could go. His nose bumped her clitoris, he rubbed it from side to side.

Amanda squeezed her eyelids tightly together. She hated herself for feeling any pleasure in what Javier was doing, but she couldn't help it. She arched her back and moaned loudly. He flicked her clitoris with his tongue over and over. She jerked. When he trapped her jewel with his lips, she screamed and came while trying to pull her wrists out of the handcuffs.

Javier slurped and eat her hungrily. When she finished shivering, he stood on his knees and walked up the bed. "You taste good, Mami. Dats why I stay going for that chocolate. I'll never admit this to anybody else, but when it comes to eating pussy you black hoes' shit taste the best and the freshest. A mafucka will have to kill me to ever get me to admit that again though." He laughed.

He stroked his dick. "Come on, it's yo turn." He placed the head of his piece on her lips and moved it from side to side. "Come on Mami. Fuck you waiting on?"

"No." Amanda turned her head away from him.

Javier grew angry. He grabbed a handful of her hair and forced her to turn her head back to him. His hard piece poked her in the cheek. "What's fair is fair. I got you right, bitch, now you get me right." He grabbed his dick and rubbed it all over her face.

Amanda closed her eyes. "I don't give a fuck what you do, Mane. I ain't putting 'nat thang in my mouth. Ain't never sucked no dick before and ain't bout to today. Dats dat."

"Yeah, bitch." Javier tried one again to force it into her lips. She rejected him. He became furious. "Alright then since that's how you wanna play shit. It's more than one way for a squirrel to get a nut." He got between her thighs with her trying to hold them together, he forced them apart and wiggled in between them. Once there, he felt around her pussy lips, finding them hot and sticky. He placed the head of his dick on her entrance and pushed forward diving as deep as he could. His balls landed on the top of her ass crack.

"Unh!" Amanda wished she could push him off of her. She hated him. He had tricked her. She felt so stupid, angry, and afraid. "You bitch ass nigga!" she screamed.

Javier ignored her. He situated himself closer to her body and began to fuck her as hard and as fast as he could while he rolled his back over and over making sure that he could reach her bottom. He pulled her right leg on to his shoulder and yanked her closer to him. "Damn this pussy good. Unh! Unh! Unh! Unh!"

Amanda tried to fight him off. She thrashed her legs as best she could. "Get off of me."

Javier forced her right knee to her breasts. Now that it was out of the way, he was able to really get to work. He slammed into her over and over. "Give me this pussy, bitch! Fuck me back. Arrrgh!" he growled, picking up her left knee and forcing it to her chest. Now her pussy was bust wide open. He watched his dick go in and out of it. Slouching and making all kinds of noises. It looked so pretty with her bald sex lips sucking and slobbering all over him. He slammed deeper.

"Unnnnnn! Unnnnnn! Fuck, I'ma kill you. Uh! Uh! Uh! I'ma kill you! Ohhhhh fuck!" Her eyes rolled into the back of her head. He was screwing her so hard. She had underestimated him. She began to shiver.

Javier leaned down and bit her left thigh. He licked all over it and proceeded to pound her out with steady, long, deep strokes. She felt hotter and wetter with each plunge. He rolled his back and crashed into her middle. "Uhhh, this pussy so good! It's so good! Fuck, bitch!" He went into overdrive, digging his fingers into her flesh while he stroked. When he bit into her neck and hit her g spot, Amanda screamed and came all over him. Javier felt her shivering and knew that she was having an orgasm. This encouraged him to long stroke her faster. He kept his pace for a steady ten minutes, hollered and threw his head back. He clenched his teeth and splashed deep inside of her, before pulling out and stroking his dick nutting all over her stomach, breasts, and thighs.

"Uhhh. Yeah, bitch. Yo li'l thick ass got that sauce. Shit." He came more and more before he fell to his side breathing hard with sweat coming down the sides of his forehead.

***

An hour later, Amanda was fresh out of the shower and starting to get dressed when Javier stepped into the guestroom with a smile on his face. He caught sight of her plump ass before she slid the skirt up her thick thighs and into place. He shook his head. "Damn, you so bad." Amanda turned around to look at him. She had a slight smirk on her face. She rubbed her wrists, remembering the handcuffs there. "So, you thought since I wasn't gon' give you no pussy that you'd just take it?"

Javier pulled a Visine bottle that was filled with water and heroin out of his Polo pajama pocket. He shook it up and took the cap off of it, squeezing the bottle just enough to emit a drip of the fluid. He snorted it up his left nostril, and then followed the same routine with his right. The Sinaloa rushed to his brain and caused him to become under the powerful influence. His eyes drooped. "Sometimes when a man wants somethin', he gotta go out and take that shit. Besides, you so thick that there wasn't no way that I wasn't about to hit that pussy," he laughed.

Amanda nodded her head. "Yeah, Playboy, okay. I see how you living." She ran her tongue across her teeth.

Javier stepped closer to her and tried to take hold of her hands. She swatted his away and backed away from him. Javier grew irritated. "Damn bitch, I thought we just had a good time. Why you acting all funny and shit?"

Amanda flared her nostrils. "Where is my money?"

"What? Fuck money are you talking about?" He took two more snorts of his drug.

"You said that if I quit my job that you were going to give me ten-thousand dollars. Well, I quit," she lied, "so I want my money." She held out her hand.

Javier laughed. "You really thought I was serious?" He started to bust a gut. He fell on the bed laughing like a maniac.

"I know damn well yo stupid ass ain't quit for real." More laughing. "You should have got your scratch upfront. Now that I have done hit that cat, I'm straight. I don't even wanna be in yo presence no more. Matter fact," he grew serious, "get dressed and get the fuck out of my mansion."

Amanda gasped in disbelief. She frowned and stepped closer to him. "This is how you're going to do me after what you just did? How bout I go to the police and tell them how the great Javier Peralta just raped me?"

Javier smiled. "Nine times out of ten, you ain't gon' do shit but run into one of the swine that I got on the payroll. They gon' laugh at your dumb ass and let me know. If I find out that you did somethin' like that, bitch, we gon' have a major problem." He took his .45 out of his pocket and aimed it at her.

A chill traveled down Amanda's spine. She backed away. "I was just playing. You can at least pay for my Uber though, right?"

"Get yo shit and get the fuck out of my mansion and off of my property. You got five minutes or I'm letting the dogs loose with the command to kill."

Amanda felt it deep in her heart that he was dead serious. She started to rush and get ready. She grabbed her purse and sprinted out of the mansion. When she made it halfway down the driveway, she stopped and looked back at the mansion. She memorized the address before she took off again.

Hood Rich

Chapter 7

In thirty-three days, after Joaquin and his crew from La Perla touched down in Miami from Puerto Rico, Joaquin had Cordoba Courts rocking. He started by selling ten-dollar sacks for five dollars. He refused to step on his product. He made sure that everything that was bagged and sold was of top quality and that the addict receiving it would be more than delighted. Because of this trend, addicts traveled from all over Miami to shop with his crew. Joaquin made sure that each purchaser was given his card and a way to contact him. He treated them courteously, respectfully, and as if they were special, and he made a decree for his workers to treat them likewise. Joaquin didn't feel above those that he served, and he didn't look at them as if they were scum. He understood that life was hard and that people needed some form of escape from it. He did the best he could at all times to provide them with that great escape.

In sixty days, he wound up pulling in twice as much profit as he did the first month. Instead of skimming back on the size and weight of his product like most other hustlers did, he took a different approach. He started to sell twenty-dollar sacks for just five dollars. He stopped cutting on his dope completely and let the word out to the streets that when they shopped with him, they would be receiving uncut merchandise. This news went viral within a few days, and his sales began to go through the roof. Because he had a consistent plug that was his father, Rodolfo, he was able to handle the heavy loads without a problem. In ninety days, his profits tripled. In four months, he was seeing five times as much as he saw the first month.

Joaquin began bringing over more and more of his people from La Perla. He moved them over in the middle of the night in small boats. When they got off of the boats, they were loaded into big semi-trucks that he rented. He brought them to the Cordoba Courts and housed everyone. In five months, the entire apartment complex was filled, and it was starting to look like his homeland. He continued this trend until he had brought over everybody that he knew. He put them in apartments and paid their rents. He gave them cars, groceries, firearms, and anything else they needed. He wanted to make sure that they felt at home as much as they possibly could away from La Perla.

In a year, Cordoba Courts and a quarter portion of Miami Gardens were populated with residents from La Perla or San Juan, Puerto Rico. The people held Joaquin as their king. Whenever disputes arose amongst them, Joaquin squashed it. Whenever there was a decision to be made that affected the community as a whole, the majority of the new citizens referred to Joaquin's opinion and his ruling was always final. He was fair and he treated everybody the same. Most of the people appreciated him and honored him with their undying love and loyalty. But then there was Jimenez.

Jimenez, from day one, disliked Joaquin. He felt that Joaquin sat up on a high horse and that everybody from La Perla kissed his ass when, in his opinion, Joaquin was nothing more than a coward. He didn't think that Joaquin had the balls to go up against the Sudanese that had taken over La Perla and because he hadn't, he took flight from their homeland like a pussy. Jimenez didn't like Joaquin or Emilia, and he recruited every other rebellious member from La Perla that felt the same way that he did. There were more than fifty of them, some were younger, and others were older. He convinced them that Joaquin was using the people to get rich in his own right. He told them that Joaquin was a coward and that he had been run out of La Perla by people that didn't give two fucks about their land. He told them that Joaquin was so good at mental manipulation that he was able to make all of them flee from their homes as well. And now that they were in America, they were forced to depend on him. He helped them to see that it was all by design.

The more and more he spoke, people started to pay attention and they began to listen to his messages with a rebellious heart. Jimenez preached about them obtaining their independence from Joaquin. He preached about them gaining their finances. He spoke about the only chance they had of living the American dream was if they went out and gained it for themselves. He preached that the only way they could do that was if they formed their own thing so they could stand up to Joaquin. He told them that when Joaquin found out that they were looking to be independent of Joaquin's so-called people, that Joaquin would be angry because he could no longer financially benefit off of them. He said that he was sure that Joaquin would try to attack them, and they needed to be ready. His multiple speeches sent the people on edge. They became fearful of Joaquin and his true intentions. They started to pay close attention to how Joaquin had every family with able-bodied teenagers or adult males serving large quantities of narcotics for him. They accrued big bags of money and Joaquin would come and collect it all. At the end of the week, he would pay each household a wage that he felt was more than fair. The rebellious members from La Perla became angry with his practices. They felt that he was getting over on them. They felt used and like their families had crossed over into slavery. Jimenez fed their minds with the is theory until it began to eat away at their brains like a zombie. His sole mission was for the people to band together and appoint him as king, then he could do the things to them that he *only* made them think that Joaquin was doing when in actuality he was not.

***

Eight months after their arrival and Joaquin had finally brought over everybody that he felt wanted to leave the island. He got them squared away and taken care of to the best of his abilities. He felt accomplished. He was certain that Martina was smiling down on him and that she was extremely proud of his efforts. He was thinking about this one Sunday morning when Emilia came into the kitchen with her robe closed loosely. Her hair was still wet from her shower. She had a slight smirk on her face. "I see you beaming. You care to tell me what all the smiles are about?"

Joaquin pulled her to him, and she wrapped her arms around his neck. "I was just thinking about my mother, that's all. I miss her."

Emilia nodded, "Well, that's understandable. I guess it's just nice to see you smiling. I haven't seen you do it ever since we left La Perla." She stepped on her tippy toes and kissed his lips.

Joaquin gripped her ass and moaned into her mouth. "Everybody is here now. I feel there is nothing more that I can do. I am free from the burden of bringing them over, that was the hard part. Before I enter into the next phase, I want to celebrate this one. I think it's about time that we hit up the city so that we can see all that it has to offer. What do you think?"

Emilia stepped out of his embrace and sucked her bottom lip. "I think it's about time that you spent some money on me, Joaquin. I've been watching all of these housewives shows, especially the ones filmed here in Miami. From what I see, I am supposed to be spoiled a little bit more than what I am. We got all of this money. You are the king of our people. Why shouldn't I be able to broadcast that my man loves me and that we are wealthy?"

Joaquin laughed. "Aw, you think were wealthy, huh? Well, what gives you that inclination?"

Emilia rolled her eyes. "I sat here with you for two days straight counting over three million dollars by hand. That was after we spent two days before that one counting four million. Now, giving the fact that we come from absolutely nothing and now we have a bunch, I would say that we are wealthy."

Joaquin looked her over in silence for a moment. He walked to the refrigerator and took out a Budweiser. He opened and drank from it. "Right now, we are currently taking care of three hundred and sixty-five people. We pay all of their rents, car notes, insurances. We buy their groceries, toiletries, clothing, etc, etc... I say that to say, the money that both you and I spent counting over the last few days doesn't go very far when you are taking care of a nation. We aren't in any position to go about splurging. It wouldn't look right. I know that's something that you don't want to hear, but I'm sorry. That's just the way that it has to be."

Emilia grew angry. "You mean to tell me that after all of the work that I've done, after the journey that I chose to take part to follow behind you, and after putting my life on the line on numerous occasions for our cause, that you're not going to spend any money on me? Are you fuckin' kidding me?"

Joaquin shook his head. "No, I'm not kidding you. There is a little more work to be done. We have to make sure that the entire nation is in a comfortable position before we go about throwing money around. If the people see that we are spending money frivolously, they will start to form these ill notions in their heads that we are only doing all of these things to benefit us. The minute their minds are corrupted, we have a problem."

"Nah fuck that, we got a problem right now." Emilia stormed out of the kitchen and into the bedroom where there was a bag of money containing fifty thousand dollars that needed to be counted. She grabbed fifteen thousand dollars out of it and stuffed it into her purse. "You got me fucked up."

Joaquin came into the room and watched her. "That money must go back into the coke budget. Whatever you just took will throw off the entire reup count. Why are you being so indifferent?"

"What is the use of having a husband that is a baller if he doesn't allow for you to spend any of the money? Right now, we're acting like we're royals but living worse than the poor of La Perla!" She stormed out of the room and into the kitchen. She began to throw plates on to the floor, shattering them one at a time. "I just don't get it." She finished a full stack and went for another.

Joaquin remained as calm as he could. "Emilia, mi Vida, you're acting so childish, I don't understand this."

Emilia mugged him. "No Joaquin, well you should. Because what I don't understand is how my sister, Cecilia, is living her best life with a man that I gave up for you. Every time I tune into one of Emilia's social media accounts, she's on a yacht, she's traveling, she's showing off her jewelry. And what am I doing, Joaquin? Nothing!" She took one plate after the next off of the stack and broke them on the floor again and again. "It's not fair. It's just not fair." She finished with that stack of plates and stepped on to her tippy toes to grab a new pile.

Joaquin took hold of her and brought her close to his chest. He turned her around and held the sides of her face with his big hands. He looked into her brown eyes and smiled. "It is better to wrestle with an angry bear than to live in a house with a disgruntled wife."

"What?" Emilia smacked his right hand away.

"I get it. You feel like we've been grinding hard and now it is time for us to splurge a little bit. If not on myself, then at least on my bride. That's understandable."

"I never even got a honeymoon, and Cecelia went to the Bahamas for hers. When she got back, Franco bought her a Porsche truck. I am driving a Toyota Corolla. Ack!" She stuck her finger down her throat to emphasize her point.

Joaquin laughed and nodded his head. "Come here, baby." He tried to pull her to him.

Emilia stomped her foot and came reluctantly. "I don't wanna come to you, Joaquin. You're going to try and talk me out of what I know I deserve and I'm not going to fold on this. You need to surrender. I'm your wife, and wives are supposed to run the show."

Joaquin busted up laughing this time. "Aww, poor baby. Come here Mami. I got you." He hugged her to his body and kissed her juicy lips. "We've been struggling for so long that I guess I lost sight of things that seem like a privilege. Things are different now. We are married, and unlike any other wife, you want what you want. It's your right as my baby."

Emilia brushed her long curly hair out of her face. "Thank you, baby. Now you get it." She stepped back and pulled out the fifteen thousand dollars she'd snagged. "So, what about this?"

Joaquin shrugged his shoulders. "There were fifty on the bed. It's all yours. It's the least I can do as appreciation for you standing by me the way that you have been. No man can stand firm and completely strong without his rib. You are my rib, and you have been ever since we were toddlers. Whatever you want, you can have. I love you."

Emilia melted and could just imagine the shopping spree that she was about to take part in. "I love you too, Joaquin, with all of my heart.

Chapter 8

It was a dark and humid night, with crickets chirping, and big rats running aimlessly through the alleyway. Mudman took his second .45 and cocked it. He'd already tucked the first one into his waistband. He took a hold of the gate with his left hand and hopped the back fence, landing in the grass. His gray eyes looked from left to right. He knelt to see if he could hear anything out of the ordinary. When he was sure that he could not, he traveled further into the back yard. He stopped halfway and checked his surroundings once again. A car rolled past the front of the trap house with its system subbing so hard that it caused the ground to shake. Mudman ignored it and ran across the back yard where he stopped at the back door and knelt. He screwed the silencer into his .45 and stood back up. He knocked on the door.

One of Javier's trusted dope boys scurried down the back steps and placed his mouth to the crack of the door. "What's up, Chico?"

"Say, Mane, I wanna cop me a little of that brown shit, ya dig. Got fifty, I wanna know what kind of play you gon' give me for that?" Mudman said with a slight disguise in his voice. He knew that this dope house was run quite carelessly and most different from what he was used to back in Baton Rouge where it was kill or be killed. For the pushers to take the customer's money, they had to open the back door just enough. A crack of the door was all Mudman needed to follow through with what he had planned.

"Fifty get you six, Papi. That sound okay to you?" the pusher asked.

Mudman smiled evilly. "Dat sounds quite nice, long as it's the same shit from earlier. Can you guarantee that?"

"Yeah, Papa. We working wit' the same batch. Deal or no deal?"

"That's one hell of a deal. Here you go."

The pusher went ahead and began to remove the two by four off of the back door. After removing it, he unlocked the three separate locks before he opened the door just enough for the fifty-dollar bill. Meanwhile, Mudman's silencer slipped through the crack. His eyes became bucked when he saw the dark black hole of the silencer, and then a bright flash from the fire spit from it before the bullet shot into his brain. The slug tunneled through the noodles and punched a massive hole into the back out of his skull. His brains flew out of it and landed all over the steps behind him. He fell to his knees trying to figure out what had happened, and by the time it became apparent, he was already dead.

Mudman stood over him and popped him twice more at point-blank range. He stepped over him and scaled the steps smushing pieces of his brain matter into the staircase. He stopped at the back door that the pusher had come out of and stuck his head into the house. He could hear Li'l Baby's album bumping out of the speakers. He eased inside and wound up in the kitchen. At the sink was a female washing her hands after eating a three-piece meal from KFC. He slipped behind her and pressed the barrel of the gun into the back of her neck. She jumped.

He leaned into her ear. "If you make a sound, I am going to kill you. Do you understand?"

She nodded. "Yes."

"Good. Now, I need you to tell me how many people are in the house, and keep in mind that the one that went to answer the back door is dead."

She felt like she was about to pass out. The pusher that had been killed was her baby's father. "T-t-three. Me and two other people. I don't have anything to do with this. Can you please let me go? You already killed my baby daddy."

"Where are they located?" Mudman ignored her pleas.

"Two in the room doing they thang, and the other one is in the living room bagging up a quarter key. We've been bagging dope all night. I just wanna go home, please."

Mudman nodded. "You say homeboy was yo baby daddy? What y'all got together, a li'l boy or a li'l girl?"

She started to shake and prayed that his questioning was because he looked to have mercy on her. "We got a li'l boy, Mane, and he ain't nothin' but two. I don't know how I'ma care for him all by myself. I can't believe you killed my baby daddy."

Mudman slammed her head into the sink as hard as he could, busting her face. He placed the silencer to the back of her head and pulled the trigger three times, splashing her brains all over the sink, dish ringer, and his mask. She dropped to the floor. He stepped away from her, and slowly made his way down the hallway. Halfway down, he came past a door. On the other side of the door, the couple inside was having boisterous sex. He could smell the scent of them in the air. He placed his ear to the wood and listened for a second. The woman was screaming and moaning in bliss. He eased away and figured there was time to double back to them. He headed into the living room. When he got there, he found a dope boy with his head buried sniffing up a thick line of heroin. When the hustler picked his head up, Mudman was standing in front of him with his gun at his side.

The hustler jumped up dizzy from the fresh hit of dope and went for his own gun that was in the middle of the table. Mudman aimed and popped him through the wrist. The dope boy hollered out in pain. He fell backward. Mudman stood over him and popped him five times in the face. He waited until he slid to his right with his eyes wide open, then he checked the pulse on his neck not finding any. He walked away. A minute later, after reloading his gun, he slowly turned the knob on the bedroom door with his pistol at the ready. The further he opened the door, the louder the pair became it seemed to him. He entered the room and got as close up to the sexing couple as he possibly could. The woman rode the man with her head thrown back while her ass popped. The man gripped her booty and forced her to take him deeper and deeper. The audio of her pussy slurping up and down his dick was loud in the small room.

Mudman stepped out of the darkness and shot her twice in the temple. She jerked and fell off of the man. The man hollered and tried to get up. Mudman aimed and popped him six times in the throat. The bullets knocked major pieces of his esophagus all over the room. Mudman checked their nonexistent pulses before he left the room and stripped the house of the four kilos of Sinaloa heroin that he knew was there. Slowly but surely, Javier would pay for his wicked ways. Mudman was going to make certain of that.

***

Emilia stuffed the last of the twenty-two bags into her Mercedes Benz G Wagon and slammed the back door. She waited for Paulina to climb into the passenger's seat before she got inside of the SUV and pulled out of the mall's parking lot. She felt so giddy. In a matter of twelve hours, she'd bought herself the wagon as a wedding gift, and then went on a shopping spree that was vindictive of a queen.

Paulina's eyes were bucked. "Mami, I swear it seems like you bought the whole damn mall. I'd be lying if I didn't say that I was jealous."

Emilia turned up the Farina track. "Girl, it's been a long time. I deserve everything that I'm getting. Besides, we're millionaires now. Why shouldn't I get to live good for a change? It's only fair."

Paulina's eyes were really big now. "Seriously, millions? You mean like dollars or Pesos?"

"Dollars. What the hell do you think this is?" She laughed.

"Oh." Paulina felt stupid. She was five feet and two inches tall, a hundred and twenty-five pounds, with brown eyes and long curly black hair. They had been off and on-again friends ever since they were little girls in La Perla. Ever since both girls had officially moved to Miami, both Paulina and Emilia had gotten really close.

"I ain't gon' lie, Paulina. At first, I wasn't so sure about this move to Miami and about Joaquin trying to take care of so many people." She shook her head. "But now, I feel like we are seeing more money than we could have ever seen in Puerto Rico. I thought it was going to be a burden taking care of everybody, but the way Joaquin has things set up, it's like everybody is taking care of us. Oh, I'm so happy!"

Paulina side-eyed her. "How much longer do you think the people will have to live with the bare minimums?"

Emilia shrugged her shoulders. "I don't know, that's up to Joaquin. I don't want to even think about it. For now, all I wanna do is relish in this happiness. I got a little more shopping to do. We'll get you a few things, and that'll be it. Tonight, I gotta sexually spoil my man. I gotta keep him tamed. Lord knows I can get used to this living." She smiled.

Paulina couldn't help but to feel envious. She was forced to live in a roach-infested apartment with no hot water and barely any groceries. Her child's father, Jimenez, made very little money working for Joaquin and they fought about it often. She hated her new life and would have rather stuck it out in La Perla. "Well, I'm glad to see that one of us is happy. Congratulations."

"Thank you," Emilia replied, only half-listening to her. She was already thinking about her new purchases.

***

"Then she told me that they are millionaires now. She said that at first, she wasn't so sure about the move to Miami, but they have so much money now that she feels stupid for ever doubting Joaquin. She also said that she thought it was going to be a struggle to care and provide for so many people, but Joaquin has found a way to make a profit off all of us." Paulina hugged herself. "Wow, what a man? They have come from such a dark road but now look at them. What a dream Emilia must be living."

Jimenez picked up the mouse trap from behind the refrigerator and was surprised to see that it had caught a huge rat. He looked the rodent over and sighed. "So, while we are stuck dealing with rats and roaches, the duke and duchess of La Perla are living like royalty. That don't seem at all odd to you?" He opened the balcony door and flung the rat out of it, closing the door back.

Paulina turned her head sideways. "What do you mean?"

Jimenez grabbed a broom and stuck it under the refrigerator. A bunch of roaches ran from under it in every direction. He started to step on as many as he could. "It just seems to me that he is using the people of La Perla to get him and Emilia rich. Every family that has a male works for him one way or the other. He rakes in all of the money, and he gives us a paycheck that is barely anything every week. That sounds like slavery to me."

Paulina crossed her arms. "You sound jaded and don't forget that it cost them a lot of money to bring all of us over here from Puerto Rico. Also, none of us pay any of our bills. They are honestly providing everything, and we would have been worst off in La Perla."

Jimenez scoffed, "His bitch buys you a few outfits and a couple of purses, and suddenly you're on their side. I guess it's true, everybody has a price." He looked her over in disgust.

"Once again, you sound jaded. You're just mad because you can't do for me like Joaquin can for Emilia. And why shouldn't she get that treatment if her man can provide it? She's been by his side since day one. At least Joaquin is not spending money on himself. That says a lot about his character."

Jimenez stepped into her face. "You sure are all over his dick. Sounds to me like you wanna be his bitch, is that it?"

Paulina smacked her lips. "I should be so lucky."

Smack!

Jimenez hit her so hard that Paulina fell backward. Before she could get to far out of his reach, he grabbed the hood of her blouse and pulled her back to him. He jacked her up against the wall. She struggled against him. "Now you listen to me, Paulina. If I ever hear you praise or talk about Joaquin the way that you have been, I will kill you. I will literally take your life from you. You belong to me. I am your man. You need to worry about the shit that I'm doing and nobody else. Do you understand me?"

She nodded. "Now, let me go." She slapped at his forearm that was stuffed under her chin

Jimenez released her. "Now, this is what's going to happen. Joaquin, that punk ass muthafucka, is going to share some of that money that he has. If he doesn't, then the golden boy will be taken up off of his throne and he will be replaced by a more worthy king. I come from the gutters just like him. Everything that he has done, I could have done it. He ain't all that, bitch, and you better know it. Now, you're going to use your plug into Emilia to get me hired into his inner circle. I don't know how you're going to do it, but you are going to do it. Do I make myself clear?"

Paulina rubbed her neck with tears coming down her cheeks. "Yeah, you do."

"Good. Now get yo ass in there and start on dinner. I got some moves to make. Oh, and I hope you kept the receipts because all of that shit is going back. We need the cash. You understand me?"

Paulina headed toward the kitchen. "Yes, baby. I understand you."

Chapter 9

Rodolfo situated himself inside of the soft white leather seats of the stretch Mercedes Benz truck limousine. The sun did it's best to shine through the dark tints of the windows. Rodolfo took a bottle of champagne and poured himself a glass. He handed the bottle to Joaquin. Joaquin took it and drank from out of it. This made Rodolfo laugh.

"Well son, how do you feel? You've bought your first major pieces of property. You now own the Cordoba Courts, and I am more than sure that with your work ethic we will be able to pay the bank back its loan."

Joaquin took another sip from the bottle and shrugged his shoulders. "Although I know the property is now mine, I still feel like you did all of the work. The bank approved your loan. You technically met with the owner and he sold the property to you, but you put all my information on the deeds after the fact. I didn't do anything but receive it. I feel odd about that."

"Well, you shouldn't. When it comes to the game, it's not what you know, but who you know. You have a connected father. Why shouldn't you use my leverage?"

"Because when a father holds his son's hand, especially when he is already grown, he only weakens his hustle. A man must learn how to navigate the slums on his own. If not, when he does have to lean on himself, he will be incapable, and the world will eat him alive. I am a survivor. A predator. I refuse to allow for your hand-holding to make me weak." Joaquin downed a portion of the liquid and set the bottle back on its ice.

Rodolfo shook his head. "You are looking at things all wrong. That's what you saw, but here's what I see." He straightened his Gucci tie and turned toward Joaquin with his suit jacket open. "What I see is a young man dead set on saving his people from the trenches. I see a man with a big heart and a lot of positive ambition. Instead of me stuffing dope into his hands as an only means of survival, I know that I should show him another way. The real estate market is primed and ready for the pickings." He smiled. "Son, with land and property it gives you somewhere to put your displaced people. It gives you power in a world that says the brown man is incapable of being anything except a low wage earner or a person that does the jobs that the Americans do not want to do. With property and land, you can control their turf and build anything that you want to build. Hell, you can make Miami the new La Perla." Rodolfo held up his glass and drank from it.

Joaquin rubbed his chin hairs. He nodded his head. "Damn, you're right. I guess I didn't think about it like that." He started to imagine the possibilities.

"That's why it's my job as your father to do it for you. Not every man is with the need of his seed bearer. There is a reason that men step into their wisdom at a certain age. Joaquin, I will never mean to step in your way or on your toes. I love you too much for that. My job as your father is to make sure that you become as powerful and as deeply woven into the financial structure of America as possible. This country only recognizes money and stature. Nothing else matters. To make the Peralta's a great and mighty name, we must conquer the game of currency, both the illegal facet and the legal. All I ask is that you trust me. I will not lead you astray."

Joaquin smiled. "Yeah, okay, Pop. I am all ears and your steps I will watch closely before I follow them."

Rodolfo hugged his son. "That's all I ask, son. Lord knows that I love you so much."

"I love you too, Pop. Now, let's get the ball rolling. It looks like we have a lot of thinking outside of the box to do."

***

Javier swiped through the pictures of the tragic murder scene that had taken place at his trap house. This was his fifth time swiping through them. He still couldn't believe that somebody had enough balls to rob one of his spots. Mudman had gotten away with four kilos of Sinaloa heroin and fifteen thousand dollars in cash. Javier was furious. He dropped his phone on the couch and turned to look at the group of shooters that were standing in silence inside of the small apartment that was located right off of Alexandria Drive.

"You mean to tell me that somebody was able to run into my shit, kill four people, take my dope, and my money, and didn't nobody see shit?"

The head of his security, a man named Trigger, stepped forward and held his belt. "Apparently, one of the pushers was in the room fuckin' when the spot got hit. If he would have been on point, then I'm sure that the outcome would have been different."

Javier got into his face. "And aren't you the mafucka that was in charge for hiring both of those clowns that got caught and killed for my shit?"

Trigger swallowed his spit and pulled his collar away from his neck. Suddenly, he felt like he couldn't breathe. "Yeah boss, but you can't always..."

Javier upped his gun and placed it to his lips. "Shut the fuck up. Bitch, when it comes to my money and my shit, somebody gon' answer whenever I take a loss." He cocked the hammer. "It's fifteen men standing behind you. How many of them did you hire?"

Trigger counted from the corners of his eyes. "Eleven, that's all."

Javier sucked his teeth. "And you got faith in those eleven men? Huh, bitch? You think those men gon' make sure that nothin' like dis ever happen again?"

Trigger nodded. Javier had moved the gun to his Adam's apple. "I know they will. Yes! Fuck, man."

"Yeah." Javier curled his upper lip. "If Trigger hired you, come over here and put your guns on the floor. "Now!"

All eleven rushed to follow his commands. They dropped their guns in a pile on the floor and stepped away from them. As soon as they did, twenty other Peralta Cartel members entered into the apartment and picked the guns up. They stood back to see what Javier was about to do.

Javier muffed Trigger to the floor. "Bitch, get on yo knees."

Trigger mugged him. "What?"

"Muthafucka you heard me. Get on yo knees," Javier ordered.

Trigger knelt and stopped on one knee. "This some bullshit," he said this in Spanish.

"Oh yeah? Matter fact, everybody that Trigger hired get on yo knees. Now!"

They reluctantly followed his commands.

Javier pulled another gun off of his waist. "You see, I am Javier Peralta, King of the Peralta Cartel, and I don't believe in losses of any kind. I don't have a forgiving heart. If you work for me, you are as close to the Reaper as any man or bitch has ever been. If you cross me, fail me, or offend me in any way, you will die. That's how this shit goes. In this case, Trigger has failed me. There is also another part of this whole thing. I am a weeder. I feel that if a person accepts, connects with, or kicks it with another person while working for me, you two, or three, or twenty whatever are responsible for each other. In this case, he hired you. That means that all you muthafuckas are responsible for his mishap." Before they began to murmur clearly or took up a protest, Javier snapped. He went down the line bucking his gun, solely aiming for heads, starting with Trigger.

Boom! Boom! Boom! Boom!

On and on it went. A few jumped up and tried to flee, but they were gunned down by his hired killers. No matter if they were killed by his guns or another, he made sure that he domed each person that ran under Trigger. Then he sent the hit for Trigger's entire family to be slain with no mercy. His killers took to the order and fulfilled it right away. Before that happened, Javier had the rest of his crew all pile into the apartment while the dead bodies were still present. He stood in front of them with a scowl on his face. "I want my dope back. I want my money back, and I want the streets painted with blood until I get my shit. Find my shit. Don't do it, and things are going to get fucked up for everybody. Point blank. The finder's fee is a hundred thousand dollars for the person that can bring the perpetrator to me. You know what? Make it five hundred thousand." Javier was looking to kill the snitch anyway, so the amount didn't matter. He also didn't want to make the finder's fee sound too ridiculous.

"Put out the word and get it done. Let this be a lesson to all of you, this is the Peralta Cartel. You are dismissed."

***

Mudman sat behind the wheel of his beat-up old Chevy Caprice with a cheap pair of black sunglasses across his face. He stalked Emilia from the parking lot of Myrtle Grove Park while she laid out on the beach. He took his high-powered binoculars and zoomed into her a bit more. From his vantage point, he saw right up between her shapely thighs to her thong.

He took the binoculars away and scanned the expanse of the beach. It was a hot and sunny day. The beach was packed and flooded with people from all walks of life. He cursed to himself and watched her through the binoculars again. He would be forced to be patient. It was all a part of the game. Only those that were veterans in the game of death understood that patience and timing went hand in hand. Emilia's time would come. Her clock was running out. He sank lower in his seat and pulled the syringe full of heroin from the console. He wrapped the thin cord around his left wrist and pulled it as tight as he could get it. The veins on the top of his left hand became prominent. He took the syringe and injected the drug into his system, groaning under his breath. As soon as the poison entered into his system, he felt like he was cumming. A bell sounded within his mind, and his eyes became lower than hell. He grew anxious. He checked his binoculars again and watched Emilia's every move.

Chapter 10

Finesse pulled into the driveway of Javier's mansion and caught him just as he was pulling the doors up to get inside of his black Lamborghini. She hopped out of her car and frowned when she spotted Fancy sitting in the passenger's seat of his car, along with his daughter, Vatican. She ran her fingers through her hair and became annoyed.

Javier met her before she could fully make it up the driveway. He had a slight smirk on his face. "You just couldn't stay away, could you?"

Finesse rolled her eyes. "Never mind that. Who the fuck is that in your car?"

Javier looked over his shoulder and spotted Fancy with her head poked out of the car door. It was obvious that she was being nosey. "Get yo ass back in the car!" He pointed at Fancy. "Damn, you so mafuckin' nosey." He waited until she followed his commands before he faced Finesse.

"You've been gon' for a few weeks now. And when you come back, the first thing you start doing is questioning me? Man, you got the game fucked up. Bitch, don't worry about who in the car." He looked her up and down. "Where the fuck you been at anyway?"

Finesse was still reeling off of the fact that he had just called her a bitch like it was the most natural thing in all of the world. She looked up at him and shook her head. "You know what, Javier? I thought that if I gave you a little time to get your mind right that when I popped back up, you would show me some respect. But it's clear that I misjudged you."

"Bitch, I forgive you." He dusted off his Roberto Cavalli jeans. "So, where the fuck was you?"

Finesse was impatient. "And if I don't answer that question, then what?"

"You don't answer that question then I'ma leave you standing here looking like a damn fool. It's too mafuckin' hot to be standing here talking to you about nothing anyway. Fuck you finna do?"

Finesse couldn't help but feel a little hurt. She thought about the ways that they'd saved each other's lives and she became sick that he could be treating her so recklessly. Besides all of the emotional things, she also had a job to do. She needed to bug his Lamborghini and switch a few wires around in his mansion, for some reason the feed wasn't sounding the greatest. She humbled herself. "Baby, I had to travel to Chicago to take care of my grandmother. She was sick with that COVID19 crap. She's getting stronger now, but I still worry about her. I know that you're a very busy man and I didn't want to bother you while I was caring for her, but I missed you so much. What are you doing tonight?"

"That depends on how many niggaz you fucked since you climbed out of my bed the last time?"

"Fucking? Ew, none. I haven't been with anybody since you. I wouldn't dream of it. You already know that can't anybody do me like you do. Why would I even waste my time?"

Javier smiled. His ego was boosted. "Shid, don't ask me. I ain't got the answer to that question."

"That's because there isn't one." She walked up on him and kissed his lips. She hoped that Fancy caught sight of it, which she did. Finesse made a spectacle by licking all over his lips and sucking on them. "I need some of this dick, daddy. When can I get some?" She reached between his thighs and squeezed his manhood.

Javier's dick began to get hard as a gang banger. He gripped her round ass and exhaled loudly. "You shaved my pussy?"

Finesse shook her head. "Nah, there's just a little hair on her, but I can shave her bald if you like. If that's how you want me, daddy."

Javier gripped her ass even harder. "Hell yeah, I do. I'll tell you what. I gotta be gone for a few hours. I'll be back by eight o'clock tonight. You go home, shave, do whatever you gotta do, then come back. I'll be ready by then, and I'm gonna fucked this pussy. Bet?"

"Nah daddy, why can't I just stay here?" She sucked his neck. "I'll go inside, shower, and shave this kitty. I'll cook you a nice meal and run you a bath before you get home. That way when you do get back, you can slip into it. I'll bathe you, feed you, and then let you fuck me however you wanna fuck me. I've been gone for three weeks and I'm yearning for some of my daddy." She bit into his neck.

Javier allowed for the chills to go all over him from the bites before he pushed her back just a bit. "Nah, bitch. I don't want yo hair all in my drains and shit. You should have shaved that pussy before you got here, and yo cooking ain't all that. I found that out the hard way." He looked over her shoulder at his Lamborghini again. "So, go handle your business and come back. I'll see you later." He kissed her cheek and left her standing feeling like a damn fool.

When Javier made it back to the car, Fancy sat in the passenger's seat with her arms crossed in front of her. She waited for him to slide into his seat before she said anything. "You already know that I hate when you call yourself snapping on me in front of your li'l girlfriends. I understand that you wanna set a precedent with them or whatever, but don't use me to do it. Damn."

Javier checked his rear-view mirror to make sure that Vatican had her headphones on before he turned back to Fancy. "Fancy, who the fuck do you think you talking to?"

Fancy looked out of her passenger's window. "Just leave me alone, Javier. I don't feel like doing this with you today." Javier kept mugging her. "Man, I swear to God. Every time I try and give you the benefit of the doubt by inviting you to come and chill with me and my daughter, I always regret that shit. You just can't seem to keep yo fuckin' mouth closed. I tobe wanting to hit you in that mafucka every time it moves unless we're eating."

"Damn, I don't get it. Why do you hate me so much? What have I ever done to you?"

"Bitch, you got pregnant. I ain't wanna have no baby with your black ass. I mean, I love my daughter and all, but I wish she was by a Latina. You told me that you was on the pill. Bitch, you tricked me."

Fancy felt a dagger go through her heart. "Did you just say what I think you did?"

"Sho' did too, and I ain't scared to say it again. Bitch, I wasn't supposed to have a baby by yo black ass. My child's mother was supposed to be a Latina. If she were, my daughter's hair wouldn't always be so fuckin' nappy. Her shit would be silky."

Fancy opened the doors of his car and climbed out. She unhooked Vatican's seatbelt and pulled her out. "Let's go, little girl. *Now.*"

Vatican's headphones fell off of her head. "What is going on mama?" She grabbed her Apple iPad and climbed out of the car.

"We're leaving. That's all you need to know." Fancy began pulling her down the driveway.

Javier came around the car with a mug on his face. He rushed ahead and stopped in front of them. This made them freeze. Javier yanked Vatican's hand away from Fancy. "Bitch, if you think you're about to take my daughter away from me, you got another thing coming. She's the only person that I care about in this world."

"Daddy, are you guys fighting?" The seven-year-old wanted to know.

"Hell yeah, we are and yo mama just lost from being so fuckin' stupid," Javier snapped.

"Don't say those things to her, Javier. What's the matter with you?" Fancy asked.

"You're my problem. You got all up in your fuckin' feelings just because I spoke my mind to yo' ass. Well, I don't give a fuck. Yo' genes were too strong. I wish my daughter had a more Spanish look than a Black one." He looked down at Vatican. "I mean, she's perfect and all that, but she could have been more perfect without yo' blood."

Now Fancy was crying. "Give me my daughter, Javier. It's not your week to have her. You still have nine days."

"Bitch, leave my property. Now, you ain't coming to Disney World with us. Go!" Javier demanded.

"No! I'm not going anywhere without her. Give me my daughter, Javier. Please." She reached for Vatican's hand.

Javier knocked it away. He pushed her as hard as he could, dragging Vatican in order to do so. "Bitch, if you don't get yo' ass off of my property, I'ma kill you and say that you were trespassing."

"I don't care. You're going to have to kill me then. Give me my daughter!" She grabbed ahold of Vatican. The little girl screamed. Fancy kept pulling. "Let her go!"

"Bitch!" Javier swung past Vatican's head and connected with Fancy's jaw, rocking her. She shook it off. He punched her again so hard on the chin that he knocked her cleanout. She released Vatican. Vatican screamed at the sight of her mother falling to the ground.

Javier pointed at his car. "Go get in the car, Vatican! Now!" he hollered.

"But why is she laying like that? Is my mommy going to be okay?" she cried. "I'm scared."

Javier grabbed her and smacked her on the butt. "Go get in the car, now!"

She jumped and dropped her iPad, before taking off running. "What about my mommy?" She got into the Lamborghini and peeked out of it.

Javier grabbed Fancy by her blouse and dragged her to the side of his driveway. He dumped her in the grass that led to the woods. He straddled her body. "Wake up, bitch." He slapped her across the face once, and then again.

Fancy jolted awake with an unmistakable pain shooting up and down her jaw. She was dizzy. She squeezed her eyelids together and looked up at him. "Why? Why did you do this?"

Javier stared at her with his eyes cold and his heart even colder. "From here on out, I'll tell you when you can see Vatican. I'm tired of playing these games with you about my child. Ain't no more going through the courts or all of that other annoying shit. I'll make the rules and I'll set the standards. If you wanna oppose this..." He stopped and saw that Vatican was watching them. "Get back in the car and sit back!"

"Okay, daddy." She was terrified. Vatican pulled the door down and closed it.

Javier came off of his hip with his .9 millimeter. "Open yo mouth, bitch? Do it or I swear I'ma blow yo' head off."

Fancy opened her mouth and closed her eyes. "I'm sorry. Please Javier. Don't kill me."

"Shut up," he growled. He stuffed the gun down her throat until she started to throw up. He pushed it down further undeterred. "Now you listen to me." He watched the vomit travel up her nose. She struggled to breathe. He stuffed the gun further down her throat until she was kicking her legs wildly and taking deep breaths.

"I ain't gon' keep playin' wit yo ratchet ass. The only reason I ain't killing you right now is because you are the mother of my daughter, but I'm telling you on some real shit, Fancy, that it's getting old. I ain't gon' keep considering that, so this is how it is going to go," He pulled the gun out and watched her gasp for air. He shoved it back into her throat again. Her eyes rolled into the back of her head. Tears ran down the sides of her cheeks into her ear canal. He pulled the gun back out and rubbed it all over her blouse. "From here on out, I'll tell you when you can see Vatican. Don't contact me about her and don't try anything fishy because if you do, I'ma make sure that yo Black ass is sleeping with the fishes. Do you understand me?"

Fancy nodded. "Yes. I-I-I do."

"Good bitch." He stood. "Now get yo ass up and get the fuck out of here. I'm serious. Don't let me catch you sniffing around my baby again. If I do, I'm fucking you over." He stared at her for a while before he walked away and jumped into his Lamborghini. He stormed out of the driveway at full speed kicking up gravel.

Fancy rolled over to her knees and began to break down, beating her fists on the ground. She felt worthless. She felt weak. She hated Javier so much that she couldn't think straight. She had to get rid of him. She didn't know how or when she would be able to, but it had to happen. Just as she was about to come to her feet, a car slowly rolled down the driveway and stopped directly in front of her. Fancy jumped up to get out of the way.

Mudman reached across the console and opened the passenger's door for her. He'd watched the entire event unfold from a chosen spot located in the woods beside Javier's mansion. "Say Shawty, I didn't know whether to call the police or to one over here and help you myself. Bout time I got here that fuck nigga was gone. Get in, I'ma take you to the hospital."

Fancy was taken off guard. She squinted her eyes at him. "I'm sorry, do I know you?"

Mudman extended his hand. "Nah, you don't. But I'm sho' you hate that cocky son of a bitch just as much as I do. My name Mudman."

Fancy took a hold of his hand and shook. "It's nice to meet you, Mudman. Seeing as I don't have a car and I am in the middle of nowhere, I guess it'll be in my best interest to trust you, huh?"

Mudman needed back into his seat. "I guess so."

Chapter 11

Emilia threw back another shot of Tequila and slammed her empty glass on the bar? She closed her eyes and threw her hands up. "Whew wee! I miss you, mama. I miss you so much. Lord knows I do." She nodded her head to the Camilla Cabello song coming out of the Tavern's speakers. She stepped off of the barstool and stood up dancing with herself. She slowly made her way to the dance floor and began to wiggle her hips provocatively. She was wearing a short Balenciaga skirt that flashed her red panties over and over. All of the men in the place paid attention to her. She saw their eyes and relished in their stares.

Joaquin came through the door of the Tavern and scanned the club. He had two of his shooters with him. Jimenez was one of his new additions by Emilia's nudging. Joaquin spotted Emilia on the dance floor and cursed to himself as he made his way over to her. She was shaking her hips and popping her back. Her dance moves caused the skirt to rise above her waist. Her panties were all in her ass. This infuriated Joaquin. He took a hold of her arm. "Let's go."

Emilia was snatched out of her zone. She yanked her arm away from him and staggered. "Get your hands off of me. It's my mother's birthday, and I'm celebrating her day," she slurred. She pulled her skirt down and tried to zoom into his face, but he appeared to be blurry to her. She squeezed her eyelids closed and opened them again.

"Emilia, you're drunk and you are making a fool of me right now. You need to get your ass off of this dance floor and into my car right now. This is unbecoming of you."

"Unbecoming? That's the word you chose?" She rolled her eyes. "I get it, Joaquin. You have an extensive Spanish vocabulary. You can speak English well. You don't have to act like such a know it all every day." She staggered to her right and caught her balance.

Joaquin looked over the faces of his two shooters. They avoided his eyes. Emilia's behavior was shameful for a man in charge. How could Joaquin be in charge of so many people when he didn't even have his home in order. Joaquin thought about this and took a deep breath. He grabbed ahold of Emilia's left arm and forced her through the dance floor with her ordering for him to release her. He pushed her into the men's bathroom, closed and locked the door. His shooters came and stood in front of it.

Emilia jerked away from him. "Nice Joaquin, you always have to show your muscle. You are the best." She rolled her eyes.

"Man, what the fuck is wrong with you, Emilia? Why are you treating me like I'm your enemy? I thought that I was your husband."

"Joaquin, how can you be my husband when all you care about is everybody else other than me? You're so dead set on building a new La Perla that you don't even take the time out to cater to me anymore. I have become nothing more than an accessory."

Joaquin was lost. "Baby, what are you talking about? I've given you everything that you've asked me for, and I will continue to do that for as long as I live. If you feel like I am neglecting you, I am sorry. I have the weight of the world on my shoulders right now. It is hard for me."

Emilia crossed her arms and rolled her eyes. "Way to make things about you. Did it ever cross your mind that today is my mother's birthday and I would lose my common sense because my sister, Cecilia, got in touch with me just to show me the display that Franco put on for her? They went on a cruise together. He catered to her the entire time. Afterward, they lit a candle for our mother and made love on a yacht. Here I am all alone while you went to make a few business trips out in New York. This sucks. I should have chosen Franco when I had the chance. Cecilia could have had you. I'm not happy. I'm sad all the time. It's true what they say, money can't buy you happiness. Get out of my way." She waved for him to move.

Joaquin stood with his head down. He felt like a dagger had been stabbed through his heart. All he ever wanted was for Emilia to be happy, and for her to feel like a queen. To hear her say that she wished she'd stayed with Franco over him was the worst thing that he could have ever heard. He never thought that those words would come out of her mouth, not his Emilia. He looked into her eyes. "Do you wish to be back with Franco?"

Emilia shrugged her shoulders. "Sometimes. I think life would have been a lot easier with Franco. He's legit, and his fortune will always be there. The foundation that we're building will crumble one day. It can't last. Though I love you with all of my heart, Franco was the man for me. I never wanted any of this. I only wanted to be loved and cherished by my man at all times. I don't like having to wait in line for the whole La Perla to get what they want before you make it back around to me. That sucks, and I'm tired of it. You and I should have remained best friends. I think about that often."

Joaquin's eyes watered. He stepped up to her and took a hold of her hands. "Emilia, I love you. For me, it has always been you and only you. I am not even capable of loving anybody else but you." He paused. "The most important thing for me is your total happiness, and if you aren't happy with me, then I am willing to do one of two things. I can either fight for you with all that I am as a man, or I can release you and allow for you to go on your way, whichever way that may be. All you need to know is that I love you, and you mean the world to me."

She shook her head. "No, I don't, Joaquin. Nothing means more to you than your precious La Perla. If La Perla were a woman, I'm sure that you would choose her over me a million times out of a million. I was convenient. Placard from your struggling past. You've never unconditionally loved me as a woman which is why you never made a move on me until Franco wanted to marry me and make me his wife. All of a sudden, you miraculously saw me as this amazing girl that you just had to have, even though you were fucking my sister," she scoffed. "Everything is about control with you from La Perla to me. Can you even remember the last time that we made love because I can't?"

Joaquin racked his brain. He couldn't either. He'd been so consumed with acquiring property and stabilizing the citizens that he'd bought over from La Perla while making a bunch of narcotic and political connections that sex had been the last thing on his mind. Now he felt incredibly guilty. "Baby, it's not easy to accomplish what I am trying to accomplish to solidify our future. Right now, I am in the trenches, and the harder I work that's the faster we will get out of them. All I'm asking for is your patience and a little understanding."

"Nope." Emilia looked up at him. "I wanna be happy right now, and if you can't give me that then I don't want this life. I'm tired, Joaquin. I miss Cecilia, and I've already booked a flight to fly out to see her. I need some time to think."

"About what, Emilia? Because if I gotta be honest, I am the one that needs some time to think. Ever since we left the island you've been different. You're not the girl I fell in love with. Every time you hear from Cecilia you act out like an immature female. I'm tired of that. Now I love you, but you have to get your shit together. We have a lot to accomplish, together, I hope."

Emilia smiled and shook her head. "I don't know how you're coping so well, Joaquin. We gave up our island and fled like cowards. Both of our mothers are dead. I no longer have a strong bond with my sister. I only see you every so often, and I don't know what tomorrow will bring. I'm weary, and I am desperate for a consistent, present, physical love. I need normalcy and daily affection. I'm not getting these things from you, so I act out. Get a clue." She walked around him. "I'm going to see my sister tomorrow. I don't need your approval. After all, I'm your wife, not your prisoner. I only pray that by the time I come back things are different."

"Emilia, if you leave for New York in search of what you already have standing before you, I don't know if I am going to be here as this same man at all for and with you when you get back."

Emilia nodded. "I hope you aren't. I don't like who you are now. I want to be selfish. I need my man all to myself. I'm tired of sharing. When you realize that, you will see who and what I really am." She unlocked the bathroom door. "I'm sorry, Joaquin. I know you're trying to do what's right for so many people. I'm sorry that you're losing what we have in the process. I mean one of us has to be sorry, right?" She left the bathroom.

Jimenez stepped inside of it. "Boss, what do you want us to do? Should I follow her to make sure that she gets home safely? Miami is crazy after midnight."

Joaquin nodded. "Yeah, do that. Please." He sighed. "It's always somethin'. Every time I get two things in order, three things fall out of whack. What a fuckin' life?"

***

Jimenez caught up to Emilia just as she made it to her G Wagon. She threw open the door and got ready to climb into the driver's seat. Once again, her short skirt was around her waist. She pulled it down after sitting in the seat. Jimenez blocked her from closing the door. She jumped back caught off guard, and her hand went for the .380 pistol in her console. "Whoa, whoa, whoa." He threw his hands up. "I'm just here to make sure that you don't have an accident. I can tell that you're a little tipsy."

"Jimenez, damn. I don't need a fuckin' chaperon. I know that Joaquin sent you to spy on me. You tell him that I don't need a fuckin' babysitter. I've got this."

"Joaquin ain't send me. I came on my own. Like I said before, I just wanna make sure that you get to where you're going safely. Where are you going?" He looked down and eyed her thick thighs.

"Not home. I don't wanna be around his controlling ass tonight. I'm going to a hotel."

Jimenez was still drinking in the sight of her soft flesh. "Cool, how about I drive you there, and then I'll take an Uber home? I promise to not tell him where you are. Besides, I'd be lying if I didn't admit that I got a li'l harmless crush on you." He placed his hand on her thigh and squeezed it ever so slightly.

Emilia lowered her eyes. "Oh really? You're willing to play with fire like that, huh Jimenez?"

Jimenez rubbed all over them. "I've been crazy about you ever since we were in the ninth grade. I've never had the balls to say anything because I knew that you and Joaquin were two peas in a pod, but you're everything, Emilia. If I had you, I wouldn't care about anything else other than you. I've never seen a woman more perfect."

Emilia grabbed her gun and pressed it to Jimenez's forehead. He froze. She smiled. "What about now, huh? How you feeling now, huh? You think you can go behind my man's back and fuck with his queen? Huh, Jimenez? Are you willing to die for that right?"

Jimenez knew that he was in too deep. He was forced to either call her bluff or up his gun and murder her before she could murder him. He didn't think the .380 was cocked. He was locked and loaded. "For you, Emilia, death ain't nothing. Try me. All I care about is you."

Emilia held the gun to his head for a while longer. She pressed it harder and harder before she pulled it off. She sighed and switched over to the passenger's seat. "You drive. We're going to the Waldorf Astoria. You better not tell Joaquin either."

"Never." Jimenez laughed to himself. He never thought that penetrating Joaquin and Emilia would be so easy. Now it was up to Paulina to make her move.

Hood Rich

Chapter 12

Mudman handed Fancy a bottled water. He sat across from her on the couch and sparked a blunt stuffed with exotic weed. He took three puffs and passed it over to Fancy. She took the blunt and began to puff away. Mudman scooted to the edge of the couch. "Say Shawty, I was able to catch a lil' bit of dat shit dat y'all was arguing over and I guess I just need to know why you let that Rican talk to you like dat, especially bout yo skin and all dat?"

Fancy shrugged her shoulders. "I don't know. Javier is just Javier. Sometimes he says things that I don't think he means. He does a lot of dope and drinks some too. I think all of those things have a way of taking over his mind."

"Sounds to me like you're making excuses for him when dat shit ain't cool, whether he under the influence or not. Dat Mane had you laid out on the side of his driveway wit' his gun down yo throat so far dat you were throwing up. Fuck kinda man a do dat to da mother of his kid? Den he dared to say that y'all daughter got too much black in her, that blew my top back."

Fancy felt like shit. "Damn, how close were you that you heard all of that?" She shifted uneasily on the couch.

"I was close enough, but dat ain't the point. Point is dis, what do you wanna do 'bout all dis shit he doing to you? You wanna go to the cops? You wanna let it keep happening or do you want his ass deceased?" Mudman looked into her brown eyes with his gray ones.

Fancy felt uncomfortable for a second. All she could think about was killing Javier. She thought that Peto would have enough brains to do it, but he failed at that mission horribly. She dropped her eyes from his and thought about Vatican. She wondered if her daughter was okay.

"What is it that Javier loves more than anything else in the world?" Mudman took four quick pulls from his blunt and handed it back to Fancy.

"I don't know, probably Vatican or his money. His money." She realized that right after she said it. Javier's money allowed for him to be a dick, without it or his power, she was sure that he would crumble.

Mudman stood up. "What if Javier was stripped of all of his money? I mean broke, disgusted, down and out. How do you think he would respond to that? Do you think it would cause him to go crazy?"

Fancy imagined Javier broke and destitute. She knew he wouldn't last long before he put a bullet in his head. "Hell yeah, he would. There is nothing that Javier clings to more than his money and power. If he had neither, he would go mad and kill himself probably."

Mudman liked the sound of that. "Okay then, that's what we'll do. We will strip his bitch ass of everythang he got, then torment him before I torture his ass to death."

Fancy looked up at him and gave him an odd stare with her left eyebrow raised. "Damn, why do you hate him so much?"

"Aw, no specific reason." He smiled.

Amanda stepped out of the shadows of the narrow hall-way of his apartment. She slipped beside Mudman and wrapped her arm around his waist. She kissed his neck. "Ain't quite what Mudman feels for Javier, it's more 'bout what he feels 'bout me. Dat nigga had the audacity to take my virtue, and he gotta pay for dat. It'd be easy to kill him and be done wit' it, but dat ain't no fun. See, Mudman here is the leader of the Cartel Killaz, so Javier's crew was on the table to be crushed after a while anyway. But with this new development, we decided that it would be better to torture and humiliate Javier before he gets what he got coming to him."

Fancy was a bit impatient. "Well, how long is that going to take?"

Mudman smiled. "Not long." He moved Amanda in front of him and pressed his front up against her ass. She leaned back into him. He bit her neck and she moaned. "I got dis shit under control. All I need to know is if you're going to play yo' role and hold us to the fullest?" He slid his right hand between Amanda's thighs and pulled her nightgown up.

Fancy nodded. "I'm willing to do whatever I gotta do, just as long as my daughter doesn't get hurt, and Javier eventually winds up going away for good."

Amanda walked over to Fancy and bent over with her ass right in Mudman's lap. Her nose was inches away from Fancy's face. "I don't understand how Javier could try and shit on somebody as gorgeous as you. He should cater to your sexy skin." She slowly kissed Fancy on the lips. Fancy pulled back a bit to look at her. She had never kissed a female before. She saw Mudman lifting Amanda's gown and positioning himself behind her. Fancy closed her eyes and kissed Amanda with passion.

"There you go, baby." Amanda licked all over Fancy's lips before kissing her and tonguing her down.

Mudman guided his dick from side to side until he sunk into Amanda's hot, wet, tight pussy. He took a hold of her hips and used them to dive in and out of her. Her fat ass clapped into his lap. Every time it smashed backward, her cheeks spread, and the crinkle of her asshole winked at him.

"Ummm! Ummmm! Ummmm! Ummmm! Awww, fuck! Fuck me, daddy! Ummmm, yes!" Amanda slammed her ass back into Mudman over and over. She ripped the buttons from

Fancy's blouse and guided her to sit on top of the couch with her thighs wide open.

Fancy followed her commands. The weed had her horny and the thought of Javier no longer being a part of her life was enough to drive her insane and into an uninhibited state of being. She slipped her panties off and opened her pussy lips with her fingers. "Do whatever you wanna do."

Amanda licked all over the fingers that were holding her slit open. She stuck her tongue through the gaps between her fingers and waited for Fancy to move them. As soon as she did, she attacked her pussy with expertise. She made circles all around her clitoris and fingered the hole with two fingers.

Fancy bucked her hips forward over and over, riding Amanda's face and fingers. "Ooo, ooo, girl! You finna make me... Unnnn! You gon' make me... Uhhhhhhh, shittttttttt!" Fancy stuffed her face into her gap and locked her ankles around Amanda's head. She fell to the cushions of the couch and came hard, screaming at the top of her lungs.

Amanda licked and slurped continuously. She flicked and kept her fingers running in and out of Fancy at full speed. Fancy became sensitive. She tried to push her off of her, but Amanda held her thighs and kept licking up her chocolate until Mudman pulled her away.

Mudman picked Amanda up and brought her back down on his dick over and over. She was so thick, and he loved it. She juiced his piece. Her calves slid up and down his waist. She licked all over his face while she huffed and puffed. Mudman kissed her lips and continued to hold her in the air for ten straight minutes while he fucked her.

Amanda began to tremble. "Unh! Unh! Unh! I'm cumming, daddy! I'm cummmmiinnnnnnggggg!" She bit into his neck and came all over him.

Mudman fell to the carpet with her, still long stroking her soaking wet pussy. Her juices oozed out of her and drenched the carpet beneath them. Every time Mudman pulled out of her only leaving the tip of his piece inside, more of her juices dripped to the carpet. He'd slam it back inside of Amanda and she would scream. He fucked her like a vicious, pussy-hungry savage for thirty straight minutes, then pulled out and came all over her stomach in thick ropes.

Amanda moaned as each jet shot onto her. She rubbed some of it into her stomach. She rubbed some into her titties, and even into her pussy. She humped up into her fingers becoming more turned on. "Ummmm, I love it, daddy. I love it when you fuck me like dis."

Mudman walked around and fed her his dick. She sucked it into her mouth, moaning around it. "Fuck, li'l baby."

Fancy sat on the edge of the couch watching them with her thighs wide open. "What about me? Y'all acting like I ain't even here?" She kept her sight on Mudman's long penis. There were veins all over it, and the visual caused her to leak. It had been over four months since she'd gotten any, and her pussy was screaming.

Mudman squeezed her thighs. "Shawty, dis ain't dat. You want some of dis here pipe, you gon' have to play yo position like a mafucka."

Fancy nodded. "I get that, and I am. Dat shouldn't stop me from getting right in this moment though." She slipped two fingers deep into her pussy.

Mudman leaned his face into her crotch and sniffed her wet lips. "Dat pussy smells ready too, I ain't gon' even lie. It's been a minute, ain't it?" He rubbed her clitoris.

Fancy shivered and jerked toward his hand. "Yes, please. Fuck me, Mudman. I need some dick bad. Please, I'll do anything." She cocked her thighs wide open.

Mudman slipped three fingers into her and finger fucked her at full speed. She screamed and began to moan at the top of her lungs. His fingers made loud sloshing sounds as they went in and out of her. "Dats dat good coochie, ain't it? Dis pussy fire, ain't it? Ain't it, Shawty?" He sped up his pace. Fancy watched as his fingers went in and out of her. She opened her thighs so far that her bones popped. She curled her back and moaned as loud as she could. "You're fingering me! You're fingering me! Uhhh, fuck! Uhhh, shit!"

Mudman pinched her clitoris and she came all over his hands jerking wildly. "Awwww! Awwwww! Fuck dis shit!" She fell on the carpet rubbing her box in a circular motion at full speed until she came again.

Amanda kneeled between her thighs with a strap on. "When a bitch this thick, Mudman, and she can't get none of you yet, dis the only way you can tame that pussy." She grabbed Fancy to her and slid deep into her with one hard thrust.

"Aww shit, bitch!" Fancy pulled Amanda down and bit into her bottom lip. "Fuck me then. Please, fuck me while Mudman makes me face him."

"Don't take it easy on me either. I see how he just did you," Fancy moaned. She took a hold of Mudman's piece and kissed the head.

Amanda smacked her hand off of Mudman. "Nah bitch, we don't use hands around here. You gon' give him what he used to."

Mudman took a hold of Fancy's hair and slipped into her mouth. Fancy began to slurp loudly. Mudman frowned and bent his knees slightly. Now at the right angle, he slipped in and out of her mouth easily. She tightened her lips and prepared for him to hit the back of her throat each time. She would gag a bit and keep right on sucking.

Amanda placed Fancy's thigh on her right shoulder and got to pounding her out with the ten-inch dildo. There was a part attached to the strap-on that manipulated her clitoris every time she went deep inside of Fancy. Within a matter of minutes, both girls were moaning, huffing, and puffing.

Mudman took Fancy's bra off of her and watched her breasts bounce up and down while she sucked him. There was no doubt in his mind, Fancy was gorgeous. With her sexy dark skin, slim yet strapped figure, and her almond eyes, she was a sight for him. It would be a tad bit difficult for him to get rid of her after they were done using her for what he had in mind. But he understood that it was all a part of the game. To him, she had to remain a pawn until he accomplished what he needed to.

Amanda bent Fancy over, rubbed all over her ass, then got to long stroking her from behind while she slapped her black ass over and over again. When it was all said and done, she'd got Fancy to cum four times and herself the same amount. They showered together and wound up collapsing in the bed on each side of Mudman. Mudman lay in the middle of the naked goddesses with his gray eyes wide open and alert. His mind was already poised for the next portion of the game.

Chapter 13

Emilia swiped the key card into the lock of the hotel door. It clicked, and Jimenez opened it. He stepped to the side and allowed for her to walk drunkenly past him. When she was inside, he stepped in and closed the door behind them. Emilia staggered to the big bed and sat on the edge of it. She ran her fingers through her hair.

Jimenez grabbed a glass and ran some cold water into it. He handed it to her. "Here, why don't you drink on this?"

Emilia took the water and drank from it. "Thank you."

He nodded. "So now what?"

"Now that I'm here and safe, you can leave. I don't need your assistance anymore." She took another sip of water and set the glass down on the bed.

"Damn, that was kind of rude," he laughed, shortly.

Emilia crossed her thighs. The short skirt rose. "Well, your tasks are complete. Now you can run back to Joaquin and tell him that you've been a good little boy. Maybe he'll crown you or up your pay. Lord knows that Paulina cries about how broke you are." She was so drunk that she didn't realize how blunt and honest she was being.

"Paulina speaks badly about me to you? Honestly?"

Emilia waved him off. "We are Puerto Rican; we talk to each other about everything. She and I are very good friends. She sees the materialistic things that Joaquin does for me and she envies them. When a girl comes from the humble beginnings that we all do, all she can see is the material things that are forbidden to her. She doesn't know that I would trade it all for what my sister, Cecilia, has."

Jimenez was stuck. He felt very small. "What does she say? Please, just tell me a few things. I won't go back and repeat them. You have my word."

"I don't need your word. Quite honestly, I don't care if you go back and tell her or not. It isn't going to affect me one way or the other. I feel when a man has shortcomings that somebody needs to let him know. If not, what will inspire him to change?"

"Right, so what does she say?" He came and kneeled before Emilia. This close, he could smell a hint of sweat and perfume. His vision was directly between her thighs. The red material of her panties was visible.

Emilia uncrossed her thighs and held them slightly open. She rubbed the inner side of her left knee and spaced her thighs some more. Her panties sunk into her gap. Her scent became stronger. "She said that she wished that she had a man like Joaquin. She said that he was a go-getter. That he had come from nothing and that now he was this major Drug Lord. She said that she envies me. She said she loved you, but you were lazy, and that you had no problem conforming to mediocrity. She said that I needed to get you a job to work alongside Joaquin. She hoped that by you working so closely with him, some of his ways would rub off on you for the better. She also says that you two needed the pay."

Jimenez wondered if Paulina actually meant these things or if she was just saying them to confuse, weaken, and manipulate Emilia into helping her to get him a job under Joaquin. He wasn't so sure, but he hoped these weren't her true feelings. Either way, he was angry at hearing them, and a bit embarrassed.

"Why are you so quiet? Did I strike a nerve?"

He nodded. "I'd be lying if I said that you didn't."

Emilia looked down on him. "It's okay, maybe you just have to find your way in life. Everybody can't be Joaquin. He is a great man. Maybe sometimes, too great. Hell, that's probably the reason why I can't handle being with him." She looked off. "I think I need for things to be a little simpler."

Jimenez stood up. "I could have done everything that Joaquin did, but I didn't because I had to take care of my mother." He lied. He knew that Emilia had lost her mother to cancer and he felt this would be an easy way to move in on her.

"Wait, your mother died? How did she go?"

"She had breast cancer." He paused for a second to allow for it to sink into her mind. "I stood beside her every step of the way while she fought that disgusting disease for four long years. Finally, it took her away from me. So, Paulina can excuse me because I chose my mother over restoring La Perla into a new land." He turned his back to Emilia and waited for her response.

Emilia stood up, she stepped behind him. Her right hand hovered over his shoulder. She closed her eyes, and it landed, touching him. "My mother died of cancer as well. Her birthday is today, and it's one of the reasons why I've felt so low. I need to be in the presence of my sister for a few days. It's the only way I feel I can get through this."

"I miss my mother so much, Emilia. Sometimes when I find myself thinking about her, I get too weak to even stand up. Paulina doesn't get it. Nobody does. All she cares about is money or the lack thereof. Ever since my mother left, all I've wanted to do was be loved and love with all of my heart. If it was up to me, I'd stay in the bed hugged up all day long without a care in the world. I just miss love."

Emilia came around and stood in front of him. "Me too. Joaquin says that he loves me, but I don't feel it anymore. Ever since we left La Perla, I've been feeling like I am more of a chore to him than his woman. I miss when we had less. It caused us to pull together more. Now that we have so many possessional, all he can think about is how to keep and accrue more. I don't give a damn about being rich. Wealthy is one thing because no woman wants to struggle, but I've been there before, and the struggle didn't break me. I would rather be in love and struggle than to be rich and neglected. I, too, am in search of the void that the absence of my mother's love has left within me."

Jimenez knew this was the right moment. He held the side of her face. "You're so beautiful. I would never be able to run the streets and chase anything other than you. You haven't changed much since high school. It's amazing the way you're physically set up." He leaned his forehead against hers. "I would die for you in a heartbeat if you were my woman, or even if I was able to obtain a portion of you."

"Really?" She couldn't help falling into his trance. She was hurting and her every other thought was of her mother or Cecilia.

"Really." He leaned into her and kissed her lips ever so softly. He stepped into her and wrapped his arms around her waist. He pulled her closer to him and added intensity to their kiss.

Emilia moaned and gasped with her mouth wide open. Jimenez sucked on her top lip, then he slid his tongue into her mouth. Emilia returned his affections for a full minute, and then she broke the kiss. "This is wrong."

Jimenez gripped her ass and yanked her skirt up and rubbed all over her warm flesh. He pulled her ass cheeks apart and trailed his finger in a circle around her rosebud. He sucked on her neck. His fingers slid into her gap. He smashed her pussy lips together before yanking the panties to the side and exposing them.

"Mmm, wait, Jimenez. I don't think I can do Joaquin like this. We're married."

Jimenez licked all over her neck and dropped to his knees. He spaced her feet and trapped her pussy with his mouth. Once he did this, he started to perform a miracle on her. Emilia bucked her eyes and placed her foot on the edge of the bed while she held his shoulder with her right hand. She started to pant loudly. Jimenez pulled her panties further to the side and went to work on her.

"Ohh. Ohh. Jimenez, wait. This ain't right. We can't. Un-nnn! Shit stop. Fuck! It feels so... Uhhhh!" She started to hump his face.

Jimenez grabbed her ass and trapped her box with his face. He licked up and down her slit, he tongued her as deep as he could. He slurped and flicked her clitoris, then nipped it with his teeth. She held him as close to her as she could and screamed, cumming all over his mouth. Her knees got weak. She buckled and fell to the ground with him still eating her like a hungry savage.

Emilia held his head and allowed for him to bring her to another orgasm. His tongue slipped into her asshole while he pulled at her clit. He switched it up and sucked her pearl with a vacuum like suction. She came again and pushed him away from her.

Jimenez stood up and pulled his shirt off. He was ripped. His stomach looked like the back of an ice tray. He stripped and pulled down his pants. Out sprung the biggest pipe that Emilia had ever seen. Joaquin was strapped, but Jimenez was ridiculous. Her eyes grew big. Now she was sure that they couldn't go any further.

"They don't understand our pains, Emilia. Only we do. I gotta have you."

Emilia scooted backward on the bed with her legs open, flashing her golden, bald sex lips that were dripping her essence. "Jimenez, we can't. As much as I appreciate you, and I feel like we have a connection, I can't cheat on Joaquin more than I already have. He is my husband, and I love him. I already have so much to explain." She rubbed her box absentmindedly and found it dripping. She blushed.

Jimenez jumped on the bed and got between her thighs. He rubbed her pussy with his right hand. "Damn, it's so pretty and juicy. I always knew that you were perfect." He slowly slipped a finger past her lips and deep into her pink cavern.

Emilia closed her eyes and moaned. "Stop Jimenez. Joaquin will kill both of us."

Jimenez added a second finger, and then a third. He knew that she was too tight for him. He had to open her up some more before he was able to slide into her body. "Joaquin has his hands full with the residents of La Perla. Why can't I be all about you! Why can't I spoil you with love and affection? Why can't I be the one that you turn to when your emotions are out of whack? I promise to cherish you. I promise to give you all of me all the time. I won't call you exhausting like Joaquin does," he lied. He moved the three fingers slowly in and out of her.

She closed her eyes and opened her knees wider. "Mmm, mmm, mmm. He says that?" She was out of breath already.

"All the time. Says he made a mistake. That he should have stayed with Cecilia. That she was less of a headache." His arm was moving at full speed now.

Emilia's mouth was open wide. Drool slid down the side of her neck. Her knees were raised to her shoulders. It felt so good. "Ummmm. Jimenez, why would he say that? Why would he tell you that?! Shiiiitttttt!" She began to shiver like crazy.

Jimenez climbed further on the bed and really got to digging in her. Faster and faster his arm moved. Her juices seeped out of her like a rushing volcano. He bit into her thigh and growled. "He doesn't appreciate you, Emilia. He doesn't. Awww, I'm so obsessed with you!" His fingers became a blur.

Emilia held her knees and fell back on the bed cumming hard. She screamed and shook as if she were having a seizure. "Unnnn! Unnnn! Unnnn! Fuck, Jimenez."

Jimenez pulled his fingers out and licked all over her middle. He sucked her lips one at a time. He traveled his tongue up and down her slit hungrily. She bucked into his mouth. Her juices continued to flow out of her. He stood up and got between her thighs, pulling himself out. "I gotta have you, Emilia. Ain't no way around it."

Emilia laid there in a zone. "No, Jimenez. We've already gone too far. I can't believe I did this to Joaquin. Despite the things that he's said about me, I still love him with all of my heart."

Jimenez nodded. "Yeah, that's cool and all of that but I gotta have you. I feel the calling for your body deep in my spirit." He weaseled in between her thighs and ran his dick head up and down her pussy lips. He shivered once again.

Emilia tried to sit up to push him away. "No, Jimenez, we can't." She nudged at his chest without as much strength as she could have mustered.

Jimenez grabbed her wrist and held it. "Look, I get it. I know you don't want to cross him, and you didn't. We can blame all of this on me. I promise." He looked into her eyes. "It's one night. We feel each other's pain for one night and then we go our separate ways. I'll only come when you call for me to cater to you. And Emilia, when you call, you will see that I am all about you."

"But we can't. I'm his wife. As much as I…" She stopped herself before she revealed her hand to him. Instead, she looked off and acted like she was about to get up. Jimenez held her down. "Then I'll take over, so I can get the full blame." He grabbed his dick and slid it into Emilia. It felt like a knife sliding into warm butter. Her pussy quivered and oozed all around his pole. She closed her eyes and moaned. When the realization that she had officially cheated on Joaquin came to mind, she began to panic. She tried to push Jimenez off of her. Jimenez grabbed her waist and began to fuck her like an animal in heat. Her thighs opened right up. She fell backward with her mouth open moaning loudly.

"Oh! Oh! Shit, Papi! Papi! Papi! Oh my God!" Emilia moaned.

Jimenez couldn't believe that he was fucking Emilia. But every time he pulled back, he looked down at his dick to confirm that it was coated in her juices. He would then stuff it back inside of her, only to repeat the same process. She was snug. He could tell by the way she was digging her nails into his side that she could barely take him. "You're doing it, Emilia! Unh! Unh! Unh! You're giving me this pussy, you dirty whore!" He dug deeper.

"Shut up! Shut up, aw fuck! Get off of me!" She sat up and bit into his shoulder. "You're taking it from me. Stop! Stop! Unnnn, shit! Stop."

Jimenez flipped her over and pulled her to her knees where he long stroked her at full speed from behind. He held her small waist. "Dis ain't Joaquin's pussy no more! It's mine! My pussy! My pussy! My pussy. You're my bitch!" He stuffed her face in the mattress and proceeded to fuck her so deep and hard that all Emilia could do was scream and moan. She started to bounce back into him panting and breathing hard. Jimenez slapped her ass and sped up the pace. "I'm finna cum in this pussy. I'm finna nut all in this tight ass pussy. Awww fuck, it's so good. It's so good!" he growled.

Emilia's face rubbed up and down the sheets. Her eyes were closed tight. Jimenez was hitting spots in her that she never knew existed. She wished she'd paid more attention in health class when she was in school. She slammed backward and implanted herself on his dick before she came harder than she had in all of her life. "Awwww Papiii!"

Jimenez smiled and pushed her to the bed on her stomach. He fell on top of her and dove back in bringing her right knee to her ribs. He rolled his back, digging over and over. He bit into her neck. "You belong to me now. You're my bitch. I'ma cater to you, and I'ma fuck this pussy just like this every day if I want to. You hear me?" He slapped her ass hard.

Emilia came and splashed all over him. She started to squirt. "Yes, daddy! Yes, aw fuck yes! Just cater to me. Put me first you bitch ass nigga. Aww shit." She came back to her knees, rocking back and forth on his dick.

Jimenez leaned backward and kept stabbing forward. He grabbed a handful of her hair and brought her round ass into his lap. He held it while he busted off inside of her with long ropes of semen. He jerked on her back. "Uh! Uh! Uh! Fuck bitch! Uh!" He fell on top of her again. They collapsed to the bed with Jimenez sucking and licking all over her neck. His dick was still deeply lodged inside of her.

"You better mean everything that you said too. I'ma hold you to it," Emilia panted. "I want shit to be about me, and me only. Don't worry about the money. I'll get us that."

Jimenez sucked the two middle fingers on his right hand and wormed them into her ass. She jumped and moaned. "Like I said, you're my bitch now. We got this shit." He slowly finger fucked her while they made out and moaned into each other's mouths.

Hood Rich

Chapter 14

By the time Joaquin made it into the apartment building, after leaving the Tavern and seeing Emilia off, it was two-thirty in the morning. He was tired, hungry, and a little annoyed with how things had transpired between him and Emilia. He climbed the stairs and made it to his floor. He was ready to pull out both of his guns when he found Paulina sitting in front of his door with her head down. Her long curly hair covered her face and fell to her lap. He frowned and became confused. "Paulina, what are you doing?"

She picked her head up and tossed her hair back. Her right eye was blackened. He could now see that her clothes were ripped and that there was even a speck of blood in the corner of her mouth. He rushed to her side and knelt beside her.

She groaned. "They jumped me, Joaquin. They jumped me when I got off of the city bus earlier. I'm in so much pain."

Joaquin rubbed the side of her face and looked her over. "Who jumped you? We'll find and kill them. Were they from La Perla?"

She shook her head. "No, I don't think so. They were black with dreadlocks."

Joaquin became furious. The area was saturated with Haitians. There was no telling who had done such a thing to Paulina. "Where is Jimenez?"

"He said that Emilia was drunk, and per your wishes, he needed to make sure that she didn't crash or hurt herself because she insisted on driving. Jimenez just wants to make you proud, Joaquin. We're both so grateful that you brought us over from La Perla. Since we've been here, you've taken care of all of the bills. You gave him a job, and it's putting food on the table. We owe you our lives." She laughed briefly. "The robbers took my keys. I can't get into the house. What a day?"

Joaquin helped her to her feet. She fell into him. She smelled like Jasmine, perfect. Her long hair fell over his arm. He slid the key into the lock of his apartment and pushed the door in once it was unlocked. He guided Paulina to the couch, then went back and locked the door before sitting beside her.

"What hurts?"

"My jaw and my head. I'll be just fine though." She closed her eyes and winced as if she were in some serious pain.

"Are you sure that you don't need a doctor?"

"Yeah, I'm sure. Maybe a little ice and a nice drink would work miracles though." She smiled weakly.

Joaquin got up. "I got you. I can't believe somebody would jump you. Don't they understand who you belong to, and what this attack is going to cause us to do to the city of Miami until those that hurt you are brought to La Perla's justice?" He came back and handed her an ice pack and glass of Tequila.

Paulina held the ice pack to her jaw after she downed half of the liquor. "I don't want anybody to get hurt. I'm just thankful that they didn't kill me. Small blessings, right?" She laughed, and her deep dimples appeared on her cheeks.

Joaquin noticed them. Paulina was beautiful, he couldn't deny that fact. Back in the day, she and Emilia had been a part of the cheerleading squad at Roberto Clemente High School. Paulina was the head cheerleader and Joaquin had a thing for her that he never explored because of Cecilia. But even so, he'd never lost sight of the fact that she was a beauty.

"I just wanna thank you for allowing me to come in here and everything, Joaquin. I didn't mean to impose, and I can only imagine that you must have had a long day."

"Well, you're welcome. It doesn't matter the kind of day that I've had, I will always put the people before me. Whoever did this will suffer the consequences of my wrath, and they will never hurt you again. I promise you that. Are you sure

116

that you're okay though?' She tilted her chin so that she looked up at him.

Paulina smiled. "I am now, thanks to you." She stared into his eyes.

Joaquin held her gaze for a moment and then thought about Emilia. "Well good. Are you hungry?"

She nodded, starved. "I haven't had anything to eat all day. We haven't been grocery shopping yet, and it looks a little rough over there." She lowered her head. "Maybe I've said too much because it's not like we're not grateful, I was just saying, well I don't know what I was saying. I'm sorry." She laid her head on his shoulder. "But I could eat though."

Joaquin allowed for her to lay there for a moment. She smelled so good to him. "Alright, I'ma go whip us something to eat, and you go and wash up. I don't think Emilia is coming back tonight, and seeing as Jimenez is her ordered security, neither is he. Looks like it's just us, so we have to make the best of it. I'ma go see what I can throw together. That sound good?"

Paulina picked up her head. "That sounds amazing."

***

Two hours later, Paulina was laid in her side on the blanket that Joaquin had spread out for them to watch the movie. She was sipping from a glass of champagne and already felt the high coming over her. Joaquin passed her back the San Juan ganja and blew his smoke toward the ceiling. Paulina took it and licked the tip of the blunt so she could taste his spit. She was hungry for him, and she needed to find an angle to penetrate the wall he had built up around his loyalty for Emilia. She blew her smoke past him. "Hey Joaquin, can I ask you something?"

Joaquin drank from the bottle of Tequila. He was both high and drunk. The situation with Emilia supposedly traveling to the Bronx was picking at his mental. "Of course, what's up?"

"And you can tell me to shut up if you want too, but I have been so curious all of these years and I've always wanted to ask you this question personally. Well honestly, I have two questions for you. The first one is, and remember that you don't have to tell me anything, but whatever happened to you and Cecilia?"

"What do you mean?"

Paulina sat up just a bit so that she could look directly into his eyes. "Well, you know, back in high school you and Cecilia were close. You two went to every dance together, every special gathering, and I know of at least three girls that she beat up just because she found out that they had a crush on you. But I guess what I'm trying to ask is, how did you and Emilia wind up together? That's a mystery that I think the entire La Perla wants to know, but they've been too afraid to ask either one of you."

Joaquin laughed. "That part." He sighed and ran his hand over his waves. "I mean, I don't know how to really explain it."

"Oh, and before I forget," she interrupted him, "I was also kind of close to Cecilia as well and I know that she is currently married to Franco, and Franco was Emilia's boyfriend back in the day. Whenever she traveled to New York, she and Franco used to spend nights doing some of the kinkiest of things imaginable. He was her first."

Joaquin jerked his head back. "What?"

Paulina saw that she'd struck a nerve. "Wait, you didn't know about this?"

Joaquin flared his nostrils and looked off. "Yeah, I did. I mean, come on, of course. Why would you ask me that?"

Paulina leaned closer so she could see his face clearer. "Oh my God! You didn't know, did you?"

"What?" Joaquin blushed in embarrassment and mounting anger.

"Holy shit, and I opened my big mouth. I'm so sorry, Joaquin. Please don't tell Emilia I told you. We can't have her making you cut off our assistance. I don't have a good man like you. He isn't as ambitious, and a string provider the way that you are. Please, we don't want to be forced back to La Perla. That island belongs to the Sudanese now."

Joaquin was furious now. "Shut up."

Paulina jumped back. "Okay."

Joaquin lowered his head. "No, I don't mean it like that. I mean be quiet, or calm down, whatever. Look, I'm not gon' tell her shit. I didn't know about any of that, but it ain't no big deal. And the Sudanese will get what they have coming to them very soon. You can bet that."

Paulina nodded. "I believe you, and I am still sorry. I just thought that you knew about their sleeping together and that Emilia was pregnant by him for a time. She lost his child though," Paulina lied.

Now Joaquin was irate. "Are you fucking kidding me?" He stood up. "How do you know this?"

"Because she told me. After her mother got cancer she began to worry too much, and her worrying caused her to lose the baby. At least that's what she told me. I don't know what's what." Paulina stood up. She walked to Joaquin and placed her hands on his shoulders for a second. She began holding the side of his face just like he had done her, to offer comfort. "Are you okay?"

Joaquin couldn't allow for himself to wear his emotions on his sleeve. He had to put up a barrier. He was the leader, and the leader couldn't be perceived as weak. Word of that would spread like wildfire. "I'm good. Thank you for asking." He looked down at her for a moment and shook his head. She was so beautiful. He slowly squats back down. Paulina followed him. "Man, when we were in high school, I used to have the biggest crush on you. I was so scared that Cecilia would find out and kick my ass too. But I swear every time I used to see you, I got butterflies in my stomach and I felt queasy. One of the reasons I flocked to Jimenez is because he always tried to act just like you. Well, that and our parents sort of forced us to be together. But yeah, you were my crush. You still are." She took the blunt back out of the ashtray and sparked it.

Joaquin looked over at her. The way she was leaned forward, he could see partway down her blouse. Her golden mounds looked so good to him pushed up against one another. He and Emilia had not slept together in nearly a month. And with the new revelations that Paulina had revealed to him, he was feeling weak and rebellious. "I ain't gon' lie, I always peeped you too. I think that you were hands down the finest girl on the cheerleading squad. You had the best body."

Paulina turned red. "Thank you." She placed a tuft of curly hair behind her right near lobe. "You do know that both Emilia and Cecilia were on that cheerleading team though, right?"

"Yeah, I know, and I said what I said. What about it?" He imagined Franco fucking Emilia and it made him want to scream. He couldn't believe that she had at one point in time been pregnant by him. That caused his flesh to crawl. He envisioned Emilia giving birth to Franco's baby and it felt like somebody was standing next to him running their nails down a chalkboard. Now, Emilia wanted to visit both Cecilia and Franco.

He wondered what her intentions were. *Was she in love with Franco? Did they still have something going on? Was that the reason she admitted to being jealous of Cecilia? Did she feel that Franco belonged to her because they were supposed to have had a kid together?* He wanted to kill somebody; Emilia was driving him crazy.

Paulina stood on her knees. She walked into his face on them. "Joaquin, I can tell that something is wrong with you. I'm so sorry that I upset you." She stroked his strong jaw. He was so handsome to her. She wished that she could have taken Emilia's place. She understood that Jimenez had sent her to Joaquin to fulfill a mission, but she honestly did feel something special for Joaquin. "Is there any way I can undo what I have done?" Her eyes were big and grown. She looked sympathetic.

Joaquin couldn't help staring at her in admiration. She was so small and gorgeous. "I think I just need some sleep. I ain't had a good night's sleep since I first left La Perla. I feel like my brain is getting the better of me."

Paulina continued to hold his face. "Joaquin, I think that the information that I just gave you hurts because she either kept it from you, or she led you to believe that there was something else going on between her and Franco. Maybe there is more to that story. I also think that you feel stupid right now when you shouldn't. You are an amazing man. You're selfless. You're strong. You have a big heart, and you are always doing for others. I think that there should be somebody doing for you for a change." Now her face was so close to his that he could smell the champagne from her tongue.

"I'm good, I just..."

Paulina leaned her face closer. Her forehead rested on his. "Stop saying you're good. You're not good until somebody takes care of you." She kissed his lips.

Joaquin backed up. "Say Mami, what are you..."

Paulina pursued him and kissed his lips again. She took a hold of the back of his neck and kissed him harder. She pulled back and went back at him. "I'll take care of you, Joaquin. I swear I will. You're always taking care of everybody else. When is it your turn?" She kissed him again. Her tongue slipped into his mouth.

Joaquin fell into the passion of her kiss for a few seconds. Emilia came to his mind, and his loyalty to her caused him to take a step back. He broke the kiss and hopped up wiping his mouth. "We gotta chill. I can't do my baby like this."

Paulina was panting. Her panties were soaking wet. "But what are we doing that is so wrong? It's just kissing." She stood up on weak knees. Her juices dripped into the crotch of her panties. Her nipples were rock hard.

Joaquin shook his head. "Nah, that ain't me. Don't get me wrong, Paulina, you're a bad female. I mean from head to toe you're gorgeous, but I can't cheat. That shit ain't in my heart. I gotta holler at Emilia. I can't even think straight. I'ma let you go and get you some rest in the guestroom. I'ma call it a night in my room. Thank you for trying to console me, I needed that. Well not all of it, but you get what I'm saying."

She was ready to panic. "Joaquin, me and Emilia are friends. I just fell into a weak moment. I mean, I love Jimenez. If you could just..."

"You're good. This night never happened. I got you." He grabbed her to him and hugged her perfect frame. "Good night."

She felt so secure in his arms. "Yeah, good night." She hugged him tightly before she released him reluctantly. She wished that Jimenez really loved her the way that Joaquin appeared to love Emilia. She prayed that Jimenez and Emilia didn't sleep together, but then again, she knew better, and it stunk.

Hood Rich

Chapter 15

Fancy appeared on Javier's doorstep at five o'clock in the morning three days after he'd taken Vatican away from her and told her the only way that she would be able to see her daughter was when he was ready for her to see Vatican. This didn't go over well with Fancy, and she couldn't help fiending for her baby girl. She imagined losing control of Vatican's custody and it drove her crazy every single second that Javier didn't call to confirm that she could see her child.

She took a deep breath and rang the doorbell. She was already imagining the drama that was about to ensue and she felt that Vatican was worth it. When the door swung open and she came face to face with Finesse, she rolled her eyes. She hoped that Finesse and Javier weren't playing house with her child. The thought was so annoying.

Finesse looked her up and down. "Can I help you?"

Fancy scoffed. "Yeah, you can help me. Where is Javier?"

Finesse placed her hand on her hip. "What you looking for him for? Ain't you got yo' own man to be hitting up at five in the morning? Where the hell are you coming from anyway?"

"Look, I ain't come over here really looking for him," Fancy started.

"But that's what you just said. You just asked me where he was. Sooo." Finesse puffed her jaws and gave her a dumb look.

"Bitch, I am looking for my daughter, Vatican. I ain't seen her in three days, and I'm worried about her."

Finesse was taken aback. "Did you just call me a bitch?"

Fancy grew annoyed. "Got damn man, is my daughter here or not? Where is my baby?!" She hollered so loud that Finesse covered her ears and closed her eyes.

Javier appeared at the door in a dark blue Fendi robe. He moved, Finesse out of the way. He mugged Fancy. "Bitch, I told you not to bring yo black ass back over here. I told you that when it is time for you to see Vatican that I will get in contact with you. Why the fuck are you here?" His robe was partly open enough to show off his muscled chest and rock-hard abs.

"I miss her, Javier. Please let me see her. I can't think about nothing or nobody else but her," Fancy cried.

"Well, you should have thought about that before you did all of that punk-ass shit three days ago. Now you gotta fall back until I tell you that I'm ready."

"No, that ain't gon' work for me. I wanna see my daughter right now, and I ain't about to take no for answer." Tears ran down Fancy's face.

Javier's face turned into a scowl. "Bitch, you ain't got no muthafuckin' choice." He grabbed her around the neck so fast that she didn't even see it coming. He picked her up into the air and slammed her to the porch on her back, knocking the wind out of her briefly. Javier began to choke her with the intent to kill.

Finesse didn't know whether to intervene or to leave the two be. Fancy had been so rude that she made it hard to assist her, but at the same time, Finesse had a duty to serve and to protect. She grabbed at Javier's shoulder before she could stop herself from doing so. "Baby, stop. You're going to kill her. Stop, please."

Javier choked and choked with his vision going hazy. He didn't like when anybody defied him, especially Fancy. He had to be in control. He felt emasculated whenever he wasn't. "I told this bitch. She's so damn hardheaded. I told her. Lord knows I told her." He squeezed so hard that a thick vein appeared on the side of his neck.

"Baby please, let her go. I'm begging you."

Finesse pulled on him as hard as she could and yet she still couldn't pull him off of Fancy. She slipped and fell on her butt, got back up and tried again. "Please Javier."

Vatican walked into the room carrying her baby doll. She looked at what was taking place and dropped it. "Daddy, please don't hurt my mommy!" she screamed. She ran across the room and fell beside Fancy. She tried to pry his hands from around Fancy's neck.

Javier didn't snap out of his zone until Vatican bit him as hard as she could. He pushed the little girl across the room and stood up. "What the fuck is wrong with all of y'all?" His chest heaved up and down. He was out of breath, and his heart was pounding so hard that he felt like he was seconds away from losing his mind.

Fancy rolled on to her side coughing loudly. She rubbed her neck. "What's the matter with you, Javier? Jesus Christ."

Javier was furious. "I told you not to come back over here. And Vatican, you gon' bite me over her? Really?" He walked over and grabbed his daughter up by her hair. She screamed. He held her in the air. The strands of her hair began to break off fast. The feeling was painful. She kicked her little legs wildly. Javier brought her up and looked into her face. "How dare you go against me for your mother? You think that me and this bitch are equal?"

Vatican swung her arms and continued to kick her legs. "Let me down, daddy. Please. I'm sorry. I'll never bite you again," she swore.

Fancy came to her feet. She slowly made her way toward Javier. "Please Javier, put her down. She is just a baby."

Javier was jaded. He felt jealous. "So, you love you love your mother more than me?" He held Vatican higher in the air.

"Please daddy, let me down. I'm sorry." Vatican cried.

"Answer the question, li'l bitch? Do you love your mother more than me?" Javier growled into her face.

Vatican nodded. "Yes, she's my mommy. You're mean. Now, let me down. Please daddy."

"Well, fuck you then!" Javier wound her back and threw her with all of his might into Fancy. Vatican crashed into her at full speed. She and Fancy flew backward and crashed into the wall. Vatican landed awkwardly and wound up hitting her face on the floor. Her left leg kicked Fancy in the face.

"Oh my God!" Finesse covered her mouth. She thought about blowing her cover and hauling Javier's ass into the station, but she knew that if she did that, she would spoil the covert mission with the Federal Bureau of Investigations, and they would more than likely demote her. She also knew that Javier wouldn't get more than a hefty fine instead of the life in prison that she was sure he was going to get once the Feds were done with him and he was officially prosecuted to the fullest extent of the law. So, she stepped back and nervously watched from the hallway.

Javier stood over both Fancy and Vatican. He pulled a .9 millimeter out of the small of his back. He cocked it and aimed it at Fancy. "Bitch, I knew it. I knew that you turned my baby against me. I should have been taken yo' ass out the game, but it's cool. Now is a better time as any." He aimed at Fancy and got ready to squeeze the trigger.

Finesse couldn't stand back and allow for the murder to happen. She pulled her service .40 Glock out of her Chanel purse and cocked it. "Freeze, Javier! I can't let you do this!" Before she could see his reaction, the doorbell of the mansion began to ring over and over as if the person were impatient.

Chapter 16

Javier stepped back looking toward the front of the house. As soon as he did, Fancy and Vatican jumped up and ran behind Finesse. Javier mugged the retreating pair while coming out of his mental fog. He pointed to the back of the house. "Y'all go back there. Now, don't make a sound. And Finesse, put that gun up! Bitch, I already took the bullets out of it while you were busy sucking this dick. You ain't on nothin'. Now go!"

Finesse looked dumbfounded. She threw her arm around Fancy's waist and ushered both her and Vatican to the back of the house. "We need to talk, Javier." She was hoping she hadn't blown her cover.

Javier pointed to the back of the mansion. "Go bitch, now."

They followed his orders. Vatican stopped and turned around. "Daddy, I'm sorry. I love you. Please don't kill me. I'll be good." She covered her face and fell into Fancy's hip. Her mother led her to the back room where they closed the door.

Javier felt emotionless, as far as he was concerned, Vatican had picked which parent that she loved over the other one and her decision crushed the last ounce of love he held for anybody. He tucked his gun and walked to the door. When he looked out of it and saw both Rodolfo and Joaquin, he became even more annoyed. "This bitch ass day just keeps getting better and better." He opened the door. "What?"

Joaquin stepped in front of him with a big smile on his face. "Big brother, I've been wanting to see you." He stepped up and hugged Javier as tightly as he could.

Javier forcefully came from his embrace and pushed him. "Get the fuck off of me. I don't know how they get down in La Perla, but in the three-oh-five, we don't do all of that lovey-dovey shit." He dusted off his robe.

Joaquin felt offended. "Oh really?"

"Yeah nigga, really." Javier glared at Rodolfo. He was about to scold him for bringing Joaquin to his residence when he saw Justina getting out of the Benz truck. She pulled down her short, white Prada skirt. Her thick thighs were well oiled and lightly glittered. Her long hair blew in the wind, and even from a distance, he could see the indentations of her nipples poking up against her blouse. She saw him and made haste to the front door. She bumped Rodolfo out of the way. "Daddy, is this him? Is this Javier?"

"Yeah Mija, that's your brother. But be careful, he's not a hugger." He rolled his eyes and looked over to Javier.

Justina ignored him and stepped up to Javier hugging his neck. "I've wanted to see you for so long."

Javier hugged her immediately and softened. He pulled her closer to him and his lips brushed across the side of her face. She smelled like cherry blossoms. Her skin was soft. He melted. "Damn, I've been wanting to see you for a while too, Justina." He ran his hands all over her back and fought the temptation to grab her ass. It crossed his mind because he was so familiar with hugging women and using his hands to fully appreciate them. He kissed her cheek. "You are gorgeous," he whispered into her ear.

She giggled. "Thank you." She backed up and looked him over. Her eyes trailed over his muscles, and the abs all up and down his stomach. She felt so guilty for devouring him the way that she was. They were siblings, she had to drill that fact into her brain, even though she hadn't grown up with him. Nevertheless, she found him attractive, once again she scolded herself.

Rodolfo cleared his throat. "Javier, Joaquin, and a lot of his people are now here in Miami for good. The reason I've finally brought him over to see you is that we all need to discuss some business and strategy."

Javier was still looking Justina up and down, secretly admiring her curves. When all of a sudden, his brain registered. "Wait a minute, did you just say that Joaquin and his people have come to Miami from La Perla for good?"

Joaquin smiled and nodded. "Yes, brother. We've been here for a few months now. I think if we all sit down and get on the same page that..."

"Where?" Javier interrupted.

"We could sit down here. I see you got couches. If..." Joaquin began.

"No mafucka, I'm asking him where you are staying. You and your so-called people?" Javier spat imagining a bunch of dirty Puerto Ricans running around Miami embarrassing him because he was connected to them through Joaquin and Rodolfo. He knew they couldn't be up to par like true residents of Miami was. Here it was all about designer everything.

"Where is Vatican? I wanna see my niece." Justina wanted to remove herself from in front of the men. Plus, she couldn't take her eyes off of Javier's body and it was making her feel weird. She needed to get laid. It had been over three months. Rodolfo was so strict.

"Down the hall, and in the back room." Javier pointed.

Justina came and kissed his cheek. "Thank you, and it's so nice to see you again big bro." She smiled and sauntered down the hall.

Javier watched her ass jiggle in the tight skirt for a while under the pretense of making sure she was headed in the right direction, then he turned to Rodolfo with the image burned into his brain. "I don't know what the fuck you got up your sleeve, but I'm letting you know right now that I ain't sharing the streets of Miami with nobody. I don't give a fuck if this clown is my brother or not. I got that Cane and Abel shit in me, straight up."

Joaquin took offense to his words right away. He stepped into his face. "You don't even know me, Javier. How can you feel so strongly one way or another toward me, when you don't even know me?"

Javier closed the door and stepped back to Joaquin. "I don't know you, and I don't wanna know you either." He sucked his teeth. "My whole life all I've heard was your name, Joaquin. This old mafucka right here worships you. He thinks that you are this mighty everything, even though I am the oldest. So, over the years, I've developed a deep-seeded utter disdain for you. I don't wanna be a part of you. I am the king of the Peralta Cartel. I stand alone. I run the streets of Miami and Atlanta. Ain't nobody allowed to do shit in these streets without seeing me and my killas. If you are now living in Miami, I'm letting you know right now that you are not allowed to hustle here unless you work under me. If you even try it, I will crush your crew. And if you still don't get the picture like Kodak, then I will be forced to Genesis yo ass."

"Genesis? What are you talking about, Javier?" Rodolfo asked, becoming infuriated.

"Cane and Abel. I am not my brother's keeper, but I will be his reaper. Blame this hate on him. He created it." He nodded his head at Rodolfo.

Rodolfo shook his head and looked to Joaquin. "My son, I assure you that I have no part in this direct hatred for you. Javier was raised to know that you existed and that you two were brothers. I don't understand his actions."

"Yeah, me neither. But guess what, Papi?" Joaquin asked eyeing, Javier.

"What's that son?" Rodolfo felt a migraine coming on.

"I don't give a fuck how he feels because La Perla is here. And guess who's the king of La Perla?" He stepped into Javier's face.

"The Sudanese." Javier started laughing. "You soft ass nigga. You ain't on shit. You let a bunch of Africans chase you from your land, and now yo bitch ass think that you're about to come to Miami and get a free past. Never!" Javier grew serious. "I ain't gon' play wit' you, boy. If I catch any of yo' people selling dope on my streets, I'm shredding their ass. I will be giving the order to strip and shoot on sight."

"Javier. They are your people. How could you say these things?" Rodolfo was shocked.

"They ain't my shit. I'm my people. My Glock, my FN with the lemon squeeze, and my bricks of pure Sinaloa are my people. Fuck them. They ain't nothin' but a bunch of cowards and a community of takers. This is the Peralta Cartel right here, Papi. That's just that. Fuck you, Joaquin. Fuck Puerto Rico!" Joaquin snapped.

He cocked back his fist and swung with all of his might. Javier ducked it and came up with his gun out of his robe's pocket. He stuffed it to Joaquin's neck and slammed him into the wall. "Bitch, I should splatter you all over this white carpet. I just got this shit cleaned too. Damn, that would be tragic."

Joaquin kept still. "Man, I'm your brother. What the fuck is wrong with you?"

Javier turned him around. He pressed the gun to his forehead. "Some of us are born to go against the grain, Joaquin. That's me. I don't want no family. I hate this blood and I hate that nigga that we call our father. I don't even look like his ass, you do. Maybe he ain't even my Papi." He looked over at Rodolfo.

"Javier, please, just let us leave," Rodolfo begged.

Javier looked into Joaquin's eyes. "Joaquin, I swear that you have never been in a war with the likes of the one that you will enter into with me if you try to open up shop anywhere up here in Miami. My advice to you is to find another city. Miami belongs to the Peralta Cartel." He placed the barrel of the gun to Joaquin's chest. "Do you understand me?"

Joaquin nodded. "Yeah, I guess I do." Joaquin felt his heart pounding in his chest. He had never felt so angry, so betrayed, so powerless. How could Javier be his brother and act toward him the way that he was?

"Well, good then. This is the last warning that you're going to get. Don't allow for this old mafucka right here to get your life taken. It won't cost me one minute of sleep. Now get the fuck off of my property, and out of my city." Javier stepped back eyeing him with hatred.

Joaquin flared his nostrils and nodded his head. "Yeah well, I guess I see where he stands, Javier. It's nice to know that too. You see, when I came to Miami, I came with the intention of getting closer to you as my brother. I felt that with us working side by side of one another that we could take over the game and make all of the opps bow down at our feet as Peralta's. I didn't think for one second that you would feel like this, or that you would go so far as to put a gun to my head. This is eye-opening. What happened to family?"

"I don't need you to make mafuckas bow down at my feet, bitch. I'm Javier. This is Miami. I am the king of it. As far as I'm concerned, we ain't friends, we ain't family, and we damn sure ain't partners in nothin'. The more partners you have, the more ways the money has to be split. I'm selfish, and I'm into me. Fuck you, fuck La Perla, and fuck Rodolfo. Get off of my lands or else." He picked up a silent alarm gadget out of his pocket and pushed the button. In a matter of seconds, the mansion was surrounded by bloodthirsty shooters of the Peralta

Cartel. They opened his front door and came into the mansion armed with assault rifles. Javier held up his hand to keep them at bay. "Any more questions?" he asked Joaquin.

Joaquin laughed. "Cool, we out Papi. Justina, let's go!"

Justina appeared at the end of the hallway with an angry expression written across her face. "Aw Joaquin, I wanna stay here and chill with Vatican and our brother. Why can't I?"

Joaquin glared at her. "Now!"

Justina stomped her foot. "Okay!" After hugging Vatican, Fancy, and Finesse, she moped up to Javier and hugged him. "It was nice meeting you, Javier."

Javier softened. "I look forward to scooping you. Don't worry, I got you," he whispered.

"Okay." She smiled at him and sulked out of the mansion never giving Joaquin or Rodolfo a look.

Joaquin took one last glance at Javier. Their eyes met. "See you, big bro. You have a nice day." He closed the door with his heart pounding in his rib cage. He had never felt so vindictive.

Hood Rich

Chapter 17

It was two days after Emilia had taken off from the Tavern saying that she had plans of going to New York where she would visit Cecilia when she opened the door to her apartment and walked inside of it. She still felt a bit tipsy from the double shot of Tequila that she'd consumed just before she and Jimenez parted ways. She struggled to pull the key out of the lock when Joaquin appeared out of the bathroom running the drying towel through his hair. He stopped in his tracks and Emilia froze for a second. She took a deep breath and pulled the key out of the lock, then she pushed the door closed.

Joaquin frowned. "Where have you been, Emilia?" He was already certain that he knew because Jimenez had been sending him hourly reports, of course, he left out most of the facts. Jimenez felt that Joaquin didn't need to know how he was fucking his wife in every entrance that she had. He kept the reports simple.

Emilia dropped her belongings on the couch and walked into the kitchen. "I don't feel like arguing with you, Joaquin. I needed some time to get my mind together, and that's what I took. I had a few days to think about some things, and I feel a lot better." She felt like she was starving. She pulled open the refrigerator in search of something good to eat.

Joaquin walked over to her and slammed the refrigerator door. "What, you thought that answer was enough? You better tell me what the fuck is going on or we're about to have a major problem in here." He looked her over. "Now, where were you?"

Emilia turned around to face him. "I haven't been in the house for more than thirty seconds and already here you are riding me like I am some gotdamn rollercoaster. You leave all of the time for days on end and I never say anything. Why do I owe you an explanation?"

"Because you are my wife, and I am your husband. You're lucky that I didn't come and get your ass. You've been gon' for a few days, and I wanna know what the fuck you did. Speak."

"Joaquin I'm not some dog, you don't tell me to speak." She brushed him off and headed out of the kitchen. "Seeing as you aren't going to allow me to eat anything in my own house, I guess I'm going to have to order in. I gotta say though, this whole bullying thing is getting pretty old, Joaquin." She looked back at him and rolled her eyes.

Joaquin tried his best to keep his cool. There was something off about Emilia, he noticed this. He thought about the things that Paulina had revealed to him regarding Franco and a strong sense of jealousy came over him. He covered his face with his hands and left the kitchen.

Emilia was sitting on the toilet peeing when Joaquin opened the door with his face red as a tomato. She looked up to him. "Damn, so now I can't even piss in peace?"

"Emilia, I am not going to go away. You're going to tell me where you were for the last few days, and what you were doing. If you refuse to do so, I'm about to do something to you that I never thought I would ever do."

Emilia kept tinkling. When she finished, she wiped herself and flushed the toilet. She washed her hands, staring at him in the mirror. "So, now you're threatening me huh, Joaquin?"

"Where were you, and what were you doing?"

"I was at a hotel, and I was getting my mind together. I smoked a little weed. I drank a bit of Tequila, and that was that. Me and Cecilia talked daily, and I even spoke with Franco. I needed time and space away from our toxic situation, and I found a sense of peace being alone." She imagined Jimenez fucking her from the back, pulling her hair, and biting up and down her back while he told her how beautiful she was. She trembled.

"So, you talked to Franco too, huh? What was your reason for talking to him?"

Emilia snapped out or her zone. "Wait, what?"

Joaquin stepped into the bathroom. "What the fuck did you need to speak to Franco about? I don't understand."

Emilia shrugged her shoulders. "I don't know. He and I have always been cool. I just wanted to see how he was doing."

Joaquin nodded. "Right." He looked her up and down. "I don't know who you are, but this is not the girl that I married." He was disgusted. He walked away from her.

Emilia stood there for a second and then decided to follow him. "It's because I'm not a girl anymore, Joaquin. I am a grown-ass woman. I have different dreams, goals, and aspirations. I no longer care about La Perla or the people from there. It's not my responsibility to care for them. I want things to be all about me. I am a woman who needs to be worshipped and catered to all day every day. I am needy because no one has ever paid attention to just me. Don't you remember how I used to always be so emotionally closed? How I didn't return your I love you's or your affections, huh? Don't you remember, Joaquin?"

He nodded. "Yeah, okay so what."

Emilia stepped in front of him. "The reason I never did was because I knew that if I had, it would open a can of worms. I knew that I'd never received that type of love and attention before and that you could never give it to me consistently, so I avoided going there with you at all. But it's like now..." She ran her fingers through her hair and pulled it a bit.

"Now, I need it all of the time. I don't want to compete with La Perla. I don't want to come in second or a close first. I want to come in first, second, third, and up to ninety-ninth place before anything or anyone comes after me. I am selfish."

Joaquin looked her over with new eyes. "What's the matter with you, huh? How can you be so self-absorbed? I can't cater to you every second of every day, as much as I want to. Do you have any idea what would take place with our people if I laid up all day long with you not accomplishing anything, huh? Damn, Emilia, get it together." He walked away from her again.

Emilia stood with her head down. "So, I tell you that I am becoming needier for you and you tell me to get it together? Really?"

Joaquin shook his head. "I've never heard you say that you were becoming needier for me. All I heard was you saying that you are becoming all about you. I don't like that coat on you. It's very ugly, and you need to do something with it." He picked up his bath towel from the floor. "Do you still have feelings for Franco?"

Emilia scoffed. She was so angry at Joaquin and how he'd responded to her that she was now looking to piss him off. "Sometimes."

Joaquin felt like he'd been punched in the stomach. "Explain yourself."

Emilia saw the sickness written all over his face and he delighted in it. "There is nothing to explain. I was going to marry him. You should understand that there was going to be emotions involved with us. You and I jumped the broom before I could fully get over him, and it was because I didn't want to hurt or lose you as my friend. But just being honest there has been times when I've sat back and had my what-ifs. Recently it's been a lot of that."

"Because I am trying to take care of other people?! You really think that is a reason to get stupid and to do all of the dumb shit that you're saying and doing? What the fuck is wrong with you?"

"There's nothing wrong with me, Joaquin. Maybe there is something wrong with you. You are obsessed with a land that has been nothing but painful to us and all of those people that you brought across that water. I mean God, have you ever sat down to think about that for one second?"

"Nah, I haven't and I ain't because I know that I am doing the right thing."

"The right thing for who? Them or yourself? And if it's for yourself, then you seriously gotta pose the question, who is really the selfish one here. Is it me or is it you?" She stopped and looked at him for a moment. "Whatever. I don't feel like doing this right now." She walked off.

"I don't love this Emilia that's before me," Joaquin's words were barely audible.

Emilia stopped in her tracks. "Excuse me?"

"Go do you, now I need some time to think." Joaquin got dressed and left the apartment with the weight of the world on his shoulders.

***

"So, did you sleep with her?" Paulina asked, handing Jimenez a bath towel as he stepped out of the shower. He'd only been able to wash himself for ten minutes before the hot water went out. He grabbed the towel and began to dry his body. "Well, Jimenez, aren't you going to say something?"

"Yeah, Paulina we slept together. We had too." He judged her facial reaction and he could tell that she was hurt. They'd been together ever since high school, and though he loved her, she was simply not enough for him sexually. He had a raging appetite. "I was able to get a bit of information out of her and weaken her in the process. I am sure that in a short amount of time that we will be able to conquer both of them with no effort."

He dried his hair and tossed the towel back to her.

Paulina took the towel and hung it up. She came back to him. "Well, how do you feel? I know that you've always said that when all of us were in high school that you had a crush on her. Now that you've slept with her, do you feel weak in any sense?"

Jimenez laughed. "You're jealous, that's cute." He continued to get dressed. "Paulina, for me it was strictly business. I know what we are trying to accomplish, and I understand that it starts with breaking the two of them apart. I am focused, and I need for you to be also."

"Oh, I am. I didn't mean to make it sound like I wasn't." She bit off a piece of skin from her bottom lip. "I guess, if I'm being honest, I just wish that we didn't have to go through all of this to reach the place where we wanna be. After spending a little time with Joaquin, I can honestly see that his heart is in the right place. He seems to genuinely care about the people of La Perla and Emilia. I was shocked because I was sure that a person in his shoes, with so much power and money, would have taken on a more cocky, arrogant approach. But he was so far from those things that it blew my mind."

"Oh yeah, and what else did he blow?" Jimenez gave her an accusatory look.

"Actually, he was quite the gentleman. I did exactly as you said and played the distress role. Instead of him taking advantage of me, he comforted me, catered to me, and made sure that I made it home safely. Beforehand, I made my move to get him into the bedroom and he declined. He confessed his love for Emilia, and I thought it was quite magical. I was impressed." She stared off into space with dreamy eyes. "I wish that somebody loved me like that." She hugged herself and sighed.

Jimenez was quiet for a moment just looking at her, and then he busted up laughing. He slapped his thighs and struggled to breathe. "Whew!" He was laughing so hard that tears were coming out of his eyes. He fell to his knees and doubled over. He beat his fist on the ground. He couldn't breathe. His stomach began to hurt. He fell on his side and kept laughing. "I can't breathe. I can't breathe. Oh shit. Oh shit." Tears were coming out of his eyes. He tried to stand up and fell back to his knees again cracking up.

Paulina was unimpressed. She crossed her arms. "What is so funny wit' yo ridiculous ass?"

"Okay, okay, okay, aw shit." He used the wall to help him to stand up. He wiped the tears from his cheeks. His face was red as a beet. "Man, damn. That fool sound as dumb and as soft as I thought he was. If he only knew how I was fucking the shit out of his wife all weekend that clown would hang himself. I hit that ass and everything. Damn, he dumb. And far as La Perla is concerned, when I become King, they gon' work for what they need and want. All of this being a dependent shit is over with. Damn." He rubbed his abs. "That was a good laugh. I needed that."

Paulina waved him off. "You're nuts. Anyway, it's good to know that you had a nice time with Emilia. I'm embarrassed for her, and Joaquin. At least I can say that Joaquin was a real man. More than I can say for you."

Jimenez shrugged his shoulders. "That bitch bad. Ain't no way I wasn't hitting that pussy. Never put a fox in a hen house and expect him not to kill something." His phone rang. He walked over to it nakedly. When he saw Emilia's number across the caller ID, he smiled. "Must be trouble in paradise because she's hitting me up already. A little privacy, please." Paulina held up her middle finger. "You're such a jerk." She walked away feeling both jaded and spiteful.

Chapter 18

Jimenez shielded his eyes from the bright Miami sun and looked both ways before he crossed the busy intersection of 22nd Avenue. Two cars sped past him as he jogged across the street and walked through the gas station's parking lot. Emilia was waiting for him in the alley to the side of it in her G Wagon. He hopped into the passenger's seat and lowered himself. "Pull off."

She stepped on the gas and began to roll down the alley with the various piles of litter crunching under her tires. "I'm sorry about hitting you up already, but Joaquin is driving me crazy. I think he suspects that something more took place this last weekend and that I'm not being completely honest with him. We haven't been talking, and he hasn't slept in the bed with me ever since I've been back. I don't know what that all means, but I'm becoming worried."

"So, you thought that it was a good idea to do what actually? Because this is hot as hell. Who's to say that he doesn't have somebody watching us right now?" Jimenez was scanning everywhere that he could with his eyes. If they were exposed, he was sure that Joaquin wouldn't hesitate to kill him.

"I don't know what I was thinking, but all I do know is that I don't want to be alone today. I need your affection and attention. I need for you to tell me that everything is going to be okay. I feel so lost. Do you think that we made a mistake?"

Jimenez had to think about that quickly. If he said yeah, then he was sure that Emilia would become too remorseful. There was a strong possibility that she would break things off with them, and then confess her transgressions to Joaquin. If that happened, then there was nothing in front of him other than a heinous death. He had to avoid that road. But if he said no, then that meant that he would be forced to cater to Emilia all day and night long. That sounded exhausting. He still needed her in order to implement his takeover of Joaquin's throne, so he was forced to keep her close.

"Well Jimenez, what are you thinking?"

Jimenez grabbed her thigh and squeezed it. "I don't wanna think about mistakes, or if we're doing the right things. All I care about is you, Emilia. You matter to me, and I am crazy about you. We need to go somewhere so we can be together, and I can make it all about you. That's what I'm thinking about."

Emilia looked over at him. "Damn, Jimenez, you just gon' make this hard, ain't you?"

"I've been wanting you my whole life. Ever since your face first broke out with all of those pimples in the sixth grade. You've been the girl of my dreams ever since then." He kissed her knee. "Whatever we have to endure, we do it together. That's what it is and that's what it's going to be."

Emilia had heard all she needed to hear. She grabbed his hand and slipped her fingers into the creases of them. She didn't know what she was doing, but she knew she needed to do it. For a man to be all about her, felt like winning the lottery on your birthday. There was no way that she was strong enough to give that up, even if the consequences promised to be dire whenever, and if ever they were found out.

***

Javier dropped the top on his cherry red Hellcat and adjusted his seat. He placed a gold .45 on his lap and looked over at Justina as the wind from the highway caused her long curly hair to blow wildly. Her edges remained intact. She smelled like Chanel perfume, and she looked just as good. Javier still couldn't believe that she was his sister.

Justina moved a long strand of hair off of her face that had become attached. She smiled over at him. "What, you don't think I see you staring at her from the corners of my eyes? What's the matter?"

Javier shook his head. "Aw, nothing. I just still can't believe you done got this fine. I swear I been fucking with some of the baddest hoes that Miami has to offer, and I ain't never laid one broad that even half as bad as you. You fucking up the game."

Justina smiled. "Thank you." She ran her fingers through her hair.

"You're welcome." He eyed her thighs that were exposed because of the short black Fendi skirt that she wore. They glistened, and once again there were specks of glitter all over them. For some reason, the sight was driving him mad.

"So why didn't you ever come down to Puerto Rico to visit us? My whole life I've wanted to be a part of you and I never got the chance, and I hated it."

"You had Joaquin. Wasn't he a great big brother?" Javier looked her over and switched lanes. He accelerated and the car shot forward.

"Joaquin is a hard worker. He sacrifices himself for others, he is always so busy and spread so thin. He rarely has time for a little sister. Since our father never had any time for me, I was forced to find attention from elsewhere. I could have really used another big brother." She looked at him and blushed. She felt guilty immediately afterward for doing so.

"Martina, rest in peace, never wanted me around. When she found out that Rodolfo had me before they ever came to be and that he lied about it, it was my understanding that she said that she didn't care about me. She wasn't going to raise a stink or cock block the relationship that he had with you guys as long as she didn't see me. So, Rodolfo kept me away until

Hurricane Maria came, and we moved to Miami for good. If it were up to me, I would have had the strongest relationship with you that I could have."

Justina nodded. "Yeah, I hope so." She looked over the road for a while. "Javier?"

"Yeah."

"Why do you hate Joaquin so much, but you accept me?" She eyed him. "Is it because you feel weird when you look at me just like I feel weird when I look at you?"

Javier laughed briefly. "I don't know what to say about that." He kept driving for a full minute. "Look, I don't know how I feel about Joaquin. My whole life, Rodolfo has always made Joaquin out to be his golden child. Anytime I was incapable of doing somethin' right, he would always say that Joaquin could do it. He would say that if Joaquin was around, this or that would happen. I got tired of hearing that. In addition to that fact, I just hate men period. I am an alpha male. I am a lone hunter, ruler, and killer. I don't need men, and I don't like being around them."

"But he is your brother. How could you not love him, but you can love me when Rodolfo isn't even my biological father?" She lowered her head.

Javier almost crashed his Hellcat. He swerved, and then straightened up his cruising before he sat up straight in his driver's seat. "What did you just say?"

"I said that Rodolfo isn't my biological father. I don't know if he thinks that he is or what, but my mother told me at a young age that Joaquin and I had different fathers. My father was supposedly killed in the war, but I don't know. Rodolfo has always done the best job that he could of being my father and I appreciate that. Without him, I don't know what type of mental issues I would suffer from." She sighed and shook her head. "Anyway, all I'm saying is that you should really try to get to know Joaquin before you write him off. You may be surprised at what type of person you uncover that he is."

Javier didn't care about Joaquin, and there was nothing that Justina could say to make him change his mind. Instead, the new development of their blood, or lack thereof, became something that he wanted to fixate on. "Alright, I'll do that for you. But it's the only reason that I'm doing it."

Justina smiled. "Thank you. You're going to see what I'm saying is true. Trust me on this."

Javier nodded. "I will."

"Now, what about me though?" She was afraid to look over at him.

"What do you mean?"

"Now that you know that Rodolfo really isn't my father, will that make you treat me differently? I was talking to Fancy and Finesse a little bit and they were saying that you could get mean real quick when you wanted to. I worry about that because I just met you and I am really looking forward to you being in my life. I want at least one of my brothers to spoil me." She laughed nervously.

"I mean is that so unreasonable to ask?"

Javier shook his head. "Of course not. As far as the whole thing with Rodolfo, I won't even bring it up if you don't want me to. That will have no bearing on how I spoil you. And as far as I am concerned, there is going to be a major competition to see who spoils you the most. I know that they can't fuck wit' my business when it comes to that department." He laughed.

Justina became excited. "Are you serious? You still want me as your little sister?"

Javier nodded, even though he had much more in mind than just that. He eyed her thick thighs and shuddered. "Hell yeah, I do. Matter fact, since you've been up here, how much money has Rodolfo spent on you?"

She thought about that question for a second and shrugged her shoulders. "I don't know. He bought me a few outfits, gave me a bracelet and that's really it. Most of his time has been spent with Joaquin. From what I overheard, they are plugging with some cartel down south and are supposed to be getting a major shipment of drugs in, that will blindside the narcotics world here in Miami. I don't know what all that means, but they've been pretty consumed with it, leaving me pretty much to fend for myself. It sucks."

Javier frowned, he wondered if Rodolfo was trying to intercept what his cartel already had set up with the Sinaloa's. "Well li'l sis, don't worry about what they are doing because I got you. I am going to make sure that when it's all said and done that you love me the most, in fact, that's what I crave." He looked her over as he rolled off of the highway and came to a halt at the red lights. He leaned into her space. "Since we're family and all that, where my kiss at?"

Justina jerked her head back. "What? What kiss?"

"I'm just saying, why not?" Javier challenged her.

"I don't kiss Joaquin or Papi for that matter."

"So, I'm different." He placed his hand on her thigh and rubbed upward taking her skirt along with his hand.

Justina shivered. "What are you doing?" her voice was shaky.

Javier closed the distance between them and kissed her juicy lips, while his fingers rubbed over her pussy lips that were prominent poking up against her panties. He sucked all over her and ended with a soft peck. Satisfied, he sat back in his seat. "I've been wanting to do that ever since you stepped out of the car at my mansion. Now, let's roll. I'm finna show you how we ball out here in Miami. Joaquin ain't got shit on me. You ready?"

Justina had to cross her thighs. Her kitty was jumping like never before. She felt like they had done something terribly wrong and it drove her crazy. "Yeah, let's roll. Where are we going?"

"To blow a bag on you, and then you and I are going to spend the night getting to know each other a little better. I'm interested in everything there is to know about you. I mean that." He kissed her cheek and stepped on the gas rolling through the green light.

151

Chapter 19

Directly after the pair of Rodolfo and Joaquin left Javier's mansion, they received a shipment from the Sinaloa Cartel of two hundred kilos of pure tar heroin. Three hours later, another shipment of two hundred pounds of crystal meth was dropped off, and Joaquin put his troops right to work. He distributed the product all over Miami Gardens and flooded the Cordoba Courts. Rodolfo had a few storefronts up and down South Beach that he supplied with large quantities of the shipment. By the eleven at night the same night that they'd received the order, Miami was rocking harder than they could have ever imagined. Rodolfo also had a group of Cambodians that specialized in the making and selling of opioids. Before he and Joaquin had gone to Javier's mansion, he'd ordered a thousand jars of Mollie and Percocets that had been remixed and made stronger than their original makeup. He knew that Javier used the same Cambodians for orders, and also the same Sinaloa drug traffickers, and his main reason for meeting up with Javier at his mansion was so he could explain to him that he had stepped in as the middle man and intercepted his next shipments. Rodolfo had fit the bill entirely, and he hoped that Javier and Joaquin could come together as brothers and fully take over the drug infrastructure of Miami and eventually Atlanta. But when Javier declined to work with either he or Joaquin, the move had put a damper on his plans. He was certain that whenever Javier found out about his indiscretions that there would be an argument and it was something that he wasn't looking forward too, but one that he rightfully expected.

Two days after all of the moves, Rodolfo got a call from Javier saying that he needed to talk to him, and he wanted to set up a meeting as soon as possible. Rodolfo agreed and asked if Joaquin could be present so they could discuss a merger of

La Perla and the Peralta Cartels. Javier declined and said that it was imperative that they got an understanding amongst themselves before they brought Joaquin into the mix. After some careful consideration, Rodolfo relented.

Javier showed up later that night alone. He came into the mansion sipping from a bottle of 1942, and he had a big smile on his face. "Papi." He held out his hand and they shook.

Rodolfo invited him inside and scanned the night before he closed the door behind him. "To what do I owe this surprise, Javier?"

Javier downed as much of his champagne as he possibly could before setting it on the marble counter of Rodolfo's mansion. He wiped the back of his mouth with his hand. "I see that you've made a whole lot of moves without consulting me. Moves that have caused me to find a new plug to meet the demands of my trap houses and call up customers. I suppose I lost about five hundred thousand dollars so far. You know I feel about losing money, Papi?" Javier walked in front of the roaring fireplace and felt the heat coming off of it. He kept his back turned to Rodolfo. The more he looked over the man, the angrier he became.

"Now wait just one minute, Javier. All of those moves were made solely because I was sure that you would come around and merge with La Perla after Joaquin and I had a sit down with you. We didn't know that you would snub us the way that you've done. And where is Justina? I thought that you were supposed to be bringing her home."

"So, you and Joaquin are a we, huh?" He ignored his question regarding Justina purposely. "That muthafucka ain't been in Miami six good months and already you're redirecting the drug flow? You out here running it to benefit him and those bums from La Perla?" He was disgusted. "You make me sick. Here you go choosing his punk ass over me already."

"It's not like that. I want us all to work as a team," Rodolfo assured him, walking closer.

Javier shook his head. "No, you don't." He looked over his father's Knight collection of swords that hung on the mantle. As a boy, he always admired them and thought that being a knight, a person under a king, was the best position to have. That was until he convinced himself that the king held the best spot. After that, the knights became nothing more than workers in his mind. "The underworld still sees you as this great and powerful man. They honor you, and to them, I am nothing more than your son. Powerless."

"Why do you think of things in such terms, Javier? Why can't you love your family? Why can't you share my covering? What is so wrong about being a prince?"

"Because a king is what I am." He turned around and stepped into Rodolfo's face. "I will never share anything with Joaquin. I will never fall under you. I will never integrate the Peralta Cartel with those idiots of La Perla. Bitch, I'm the only leader. Y'all need to bow to me. Be my knights or get the fuck off of the board!" He stepped closer and brushed his forehead against Rodolfo's. "What's it gon' be, old man?"

Rodolfo was furious. He began to shake. He stepped away from Javier and turned his back to his son. "Where is Justina? I am worried about her."

"That ain't yo bidness. Answer my question?" Javier slowly slipped one of the swords out of its sheath. "Bow to me, or else."

"Not my business." He turned around.

Javier zipped the blade and held it to Rodolfo's throat. "Justina belongs to me now. I ain't never been able to love nothing or nobody. For some reason since our coupling would be so wrong and so ill-advised, it makes me want her. And ain't no reason for you yo worry about it, seeing as you aren't her real father anyway."

Rodolfo's eyes grew big. "Not her real father? Javier, what are you talking about? You're losing your mind and I'm tired of it." He frowned and tried to smack the sword out of Javier's hand with the intention of rushing him directly afterward.

Javier sidestepped him and kicked him in the ass. Rodolfo stumbled forward and fell against the marble counter. Javier felt like it was now or never. "As long as you're alive, they will never respect my slot. For a prince to become a king, the King must die!" He raised the sword over his head and ran full speed at Rodolfo with no mercy and no regard for his life.

Rodolfo struggled to pull his gun out of his waistband. "Wait, son, don't do this." He yanked the gun from his belt and cocked it. He aimed at Javier and closed his eyes.

***

Jimenez threw Emilia up against the wall and picked her up. He slipped his dick back into her and bounced her up and down while she moaned at the top of her lungs and licked all over his face. She bit into his shoulder and begged him to fuck her harder. Jimenez fell to the floor with her, bucking his back digging deeper and deeper into her. Her pussy kept getting better and better. He groaned and shot his seed deep within her. He rolled on to his back, Emilia slipped off of him and sucked him into her mouth deepthroating him loudly while she played between her thighs feeling his seed leaking out of her. "You finna let me ride this dick now? I'ma make you tap out, and then we'll discuss what you're were telling me about, but not before then." She got him as hard as he could be and then jumped on top of him sliding back with her mouth opened wide.

"Long as you gon' help me get to the top, I belong to you, Emilia. It's all about you."

Emilia screamed and fucked him harder. "Awww, say it again, baby!" She bounced harder on him.

"It's all about you!" Jimenez groaned holding her ass.

***

After slipping through the bathroom window, Joaquin stood in the short hallway watching the entire scene with his heart tearing in two. This, for him, was a betrayal on another level. He pulled his black leather gloves taut on his fingers and became irate. He couldn't believe that his beloved Emilia would cross him in such a fashion. He felt like a fool. Memories of their past started to go through his mind. He grew even sicker. *Where had everything gone downhill?* He wondered. He watched the pair continue with their aggressive lovemaking, and it only hurt him all the more. He had made a mistake. He tilted his head to the ceiling and spoke loud enough for only himself to hear. He knew what came next and he felt a way about it only for a split second. "Mama, forgive me for what I'm about to do." He pulled an Army knife from his waistband and slowly walked into the bedroom with tears of a savage coming down his cheeks. His heart grew colder with every step that he took.

To Be Continued...
Dope Gods 3
Coming Soon

Submission Guideline

Submit the first three chapters of your completed manuscript to ldpsubmissions@gmail.com, subject line: Your book's title. The manuscript must be in a .doc file and sent as an attachment. Document should be in Times New Roman, double spaced and in size 12 font. Also, provide your synopsis and full contact information. If sending multiple submissions, they must each be in a separate email.

Have a story but no way to send it electronically? You can still submit to LDP/Ca$h Presents. Send in the first three chapters, written or typed, of your completed manuscript to:

LDP: Submissions Dept
Po Box 944
Stockbridge, Ga 30281

DO NOT send original manuscript. Must be a duplicate.

Provide your synopsis and a cover letter containing your full contact information.

Thanks for considering LDP and Ca$h Presents.

<u>Coming Soon from Lock Down Publications/Ca$h Presents</u>

BOW DOWN TO MY GANGSTA
By **Ca$h**
TORN BETWEEN TWO
By **Coffee**
THE STREETS STAINED MY SOUL **II**
By **Marcellus Allen**
BLOOD OF A BOSS **VI**
SHADOWS OF THE GAME II
By **Askari**
LOYAL TO THE GAME **IV**
By **T.J. & Jelissa**
A DOPEBOY'S PRAYER **II**
By **Eddie "Wolf" Lee**
IF LOVING YOU IS WRONG… **III**
By **Jelissa**
TRUE SAVAGE **VII**
MIDNIGHT CARTEL III
DOPE BOY MAGIC IV
CITY OF KINGZ II
By **Chris Green**
BLAST FOR ME **III**
A SAVAGE DOPEBOY III
CUTTHROAT MAFIA II
By **Ghost**
A HUSTLER'S DECEIT III

KILL ZONE **II**

BAE BELONGS TO ME III

A DOPE BOY'S QUEEN II

By **Aryanna**

COKE KINGS V

KING OF THE TRAP II

By **T.J. Edwards**

GORILLAZ IN THE BAY V

De'Kari

THE STREETS ARE CALLING II

Duquie Wilson

KINGPIN KILLAZ IV

STREET KINGS III

PAID IN BLOOD III

CARTEL KILLAZ IV

DOPE GODS III

Hood Rich

SINS OF A HUSTLA II

ASAD

KINGZ OF THE GAME V

Playa Ray

SLAUGHTER GANG IV

RUTHLESS HEART IV

By Willie Slaughter

THE HEART OF A SAVAGE III

By Jibril Williams

FUK SHYT II

By Blakk Diamond
FEAR MY GANGSTA 5
THE REALEST KILLAZ II
By Tranay Adams
TRAP GOD II
By Troublesome
YAYO IV
A SHOOTER'S AMBITION III
By S. Allen
GHOST MOB
Stilloan Robinson
KINGPIN DREAMS III
By Paper Boi Rari
CREAM
By Yolanda Moore
SON OF A DOPE FIEND II
By Renta
FOREVER GANGSTA II
GLOCKS ON SATIN SHEETS III
By Adrian Dulan
LOYALTY AIN'T PROMISED II
By Keith Williams
THE PRICE YOU PAY FOR LOVE II
DOPE GIRL MAGIC III
By Destiny Skai
CONFESSIONS OF A GANGSTA II
By Nicholas Lock

I'M NOTHING WITHOUT HIS LOVE II
By Monet Dragun
CAUGHT UP IN THE LIFE III
By Robert Baptiste
LIFE OF A SAVAGE IV
A GANGSTA'S QUR'AN II
By **Romell Tukes**
QUIET MONEY III
THUG LIFE II
By **Trai'Quan**
THE STREETS MADE ME III
By **Larry D. Wright**
THE ULTIMATE SACRIFICE VI
IF YOU CROSS ME ONCE II
ANGEL III
By **Anthony Fields**
THE LIFE OF A HOOD STAR
By Ca$h & Rashia Wilson
FRIEND OR FOE II
By **Mimi**
SAVAGE STORMS II
By **Meesha**

<ins>Available Now</ins>

RESTRAINING ORDER **I & II**
By **CA$H & Coffee**
LOVE KNOWS NO BOUNDARIES **I II & III**
By **Coffee**
RAISED AS A GOON I, II, III & IV
BRED BY THE SLUMS I, II, III
BLAST FOR ME I & II
ROTTEN TO THE CORE I II III
A BRONX TALE I, II, III
DUFFEL BAG CARTEL I II III IV
HEARTLESS GOON I II III IV
A SAVAGE DOPEBOY I II
HEARTLESS GOON I II III
DRUG LORDS I II III
CUTTHROAT MAFIA
By **Ghost**
LAY IT DOWN **I & II**
LAST OF A DYING BREED
BLOOD STAINS OF A SHOTTA I & II III
By **Jamaica**
LOYAL TO THE GAME I II III
LIFE OF SIN I, II III
By **TJ & Jelissa**
BLOODY COMMAS I & II
SKI MASK CARTEL I II & III
KING OF NEW YORK I II,III IV V

RISE TO POWER I II III

COKE KINGS I II III IV

BORN HEARTLESS I II III IV

KING OF THE TRAP

By **T.J. Edwards**

IF LOVING HIM IS WRONG…I & II

LOVE ME EVEN WHEN IT HURTS I II III

By **Jelissa**

WHEN THE STREETS CLAP BACK I & II III

THE HEART OF A SAVAGE I II

By **Jibril Williams**

A DISTINGUISHED THUG STOLE MY HEART I II & III

LOVE SHOULDN'T HURT I II III IV

RENEGADE BOYS I II III IV

PAID IN KARMA I II III

SAVAGE STORMS

By **Meesha**

A GANGSTER'S CODE I &, II III

A GANGSTER'S SYN I II III

THE SAVAGE LIFE I II III

CHAINED TO THE STREETS I II III

By J-Blunt

PUSH IT TO THE LIMIT

By **Bre' Hayes**

BLOOD OF A BOSS **I, II, III, IV, V**

SHADOWS OF THE GAME

By **Askari**

THE STREETS BLEED MURDER **I, II & III**

THE HEART OF A GANGSTA I II& III

By **Jerry Jackson**

CUM FOR ME I II III IV V

An **LDP Erotica Collaboration**

BRIDE OF A HUSTLA **I II & II**

THE FETTI GIRLS **I, II& III**

CORRUPTED BY A GANGSTA I, II III, IV

BLINDED BY HIS LOVE

THE PRICE YOU PAY FOR LOVE

DOPE GIRL MAGIC I II

By **Destiny Skai**

WHEN A GOOD GIRL GOES BAD

By **Adrienne**

THE COST OF LOYALTY I II III

By Kweli

A GANGSTER'S REVENGE **I II III & IV**

THE BOSS MAN'S DAUGHTERS I II III IV V

A SAVAGE LOVE **I & II**

BAE BELONGS TO ME I II

A HUSTLER'S DECEIT I, II, III

WHAT BAD BITCHES DO I, II, III

SOUL OF A MONSTER I II III

KILL ZONE

A DOPE BOY'S QUEEN

By **Aryanna**

A KINGPIN'S AMBITON

A KINGPIN'S AMBITION **II**

I MURDER FOR THE DOUGH

By **Ambitious**

TRUE SAVAGE I II III IV V VI

DOPE BOY MAGIC I, II, III

MIDNIGHT CARTEL I II

CITY OF KINGZ

By **Chris Green**

A DOPEBOY'S PRAYER

By **Eddie "Wolf" Lee**

THE KING CARTEL **I, II & III**

By **Frank Gresham**

THESE NIGGAS AIN'T LOYAL **I, II & III**

By **Nikki Tee**

GANGSTA SHYT **I II &III**

By **CATO**

THE ULTIMATE BETRAYAL

By **Phoenix**

BOSS'N UP **I , II & III**

By **Royal Nicole**

I LOVE YOU TO DEATH

By Destiny J

I RIDE FOR MY HITTA

I STILL RIDE FOR MY HITTA

By **Misty Holt**

LOVE & CHASIN' PAPER

By **Qay Crockett**

TO DIE IN VAIN

SINS OF A HUSTLA

By **ASAD**

BROOKLYN HUSTLAZ

By **Boogsy Morina**

BROOKLYN ON LOCK I & II

By **Sonovia**

GANGSTA CITY

By **Teddy Duke**

A DRUG KING AND HIS DIAMOND I & II III

A DOPEMAN'S RICHES

HER MAN, MINE'S TOO I, II

CASH MONEY HO'S

By Nicole Goosby

TRAPHOUSE KING **I II & III**

KINGPIN KILLAZ I II III

STREET KINGS I II

PAID IN BLOOD **I II**

CARTEL KILLAZ I II III

DOPE GODS I II

By **Hood Rich**

LIPSTICK KILLAH **I, II, III**

CRIME OF PASSION I II & III

FRIEND OR FOE

By **Mimi**

STEADY MOBBN' **I, II, III**

THE STREETS STAINED MY SOUL

Hood Rich

By **Marcellus Allen**

WHO SHOT YA **I, II, III**

SON OF A DOPE FIEND

Renta

GORILLAZ IN THE BAY **I II III IV**

TEARS OF A GANGSTA I II

DE'KARI

TRIGGADALE I II III

Elijah R. Freeman

GOD BLESS THE TRAPPERS I, II, III

THESE SCANDALOUS STREETS I, II, III

FEAR MY GANGSTA I, II, III IV

THESE STREETS DON'T LOVE NOBODY I, II

BURY ME A G I, II, III, IV, V

A GANGSTA'S EMPIRE I, II, III, IV

THE DOPEMAN'S BODYGAURD I II

THE REALEST KILLAZ

Tranay Adams

THE STREETS ARE CALLING

Duquie Wilson

MARRIED TO A BOSS... I II III

By Destiny Skai & Chris Green

KINGZ OF THE GAME I II III IV

Playa Ray

SLAUGHTER GANG I II III

RUTHLESS HEART I II III

By Willie Slaughter

FUK SHYT

By Blakk Diamond

DON'T F#CK WITH MY HEART I II

By Linnea

ADDICTED TO THE DRAMA I II III

By Jamila

YAYO I II III

A SHOOTER'S AMBITION I II

By S. Allen

TRAP GOD

By Troublesome

FOREVER GANGSTA

GLOCKS ON SATIN SHEETS I II

By Adrian Dulan

TOE TAGZ I II III

By Ah'Million

KINGPIN DREAMS I II

By Paper Boi Rari

CONFESSIONS OF A GANGSTA

By Nicholas Lock

I'M NOTHING WITHOUT HIS LOVE

By Monet Dragun

CAUGHT UP IN THE LIFE I II

By Robert Baptiste

NEW TO THE GAME I II III

By **Malik D. Rice**

LIFE OF A SAVAGE I II III

A GANGSTA'S QUR'AN

By **Romell Tukes**

LOYALTY AIN'T PROMISED

By Keith Williams

QUIET MONEY I II

THUG LIFE

By **Trai'Quan**

THE STREETS MADE ME I II

By **Larry D. Wright**

THE ULTIMATE SACRIFICE I, II, III, IV, V

KHADIFI

IF YOU CROSS ME ONCE

ANGEL I II

By **Anthony Fields**

THE LIFE OF A HOOD STAR

By Ca$h & Rashia Wilson

<u>BOOKS BY LDP'S CEO, CA$H</u>

<u>TRUST IN NO MAN</u>

<u>TRUST IN NO MAN 2</u>

<u>TRUST IN NO MAN 3</u>

<u>BONDED BY BLOOD</u>

<u>SHORTY GOT A THUG</u>

<u>THUGS CRY</u>

<u>THUGS CRY 2</u>

<u>THUGS CRY 3</u>

<u>TRUST NO BITCH</u>

<u>TRUST NO BITCH 2</u>

<u>TRUST NO BITCH 3</u>

<u>TIL MY CASKET DROPS</u>

<u>RESTRAINING ORDER</u>

<u>RESTRAINING ORDER 2</u>

<u>IN LOVE WITH A CONVICT</u>

<u>LIFE OF A HOOD STAR</u>

<u>Coming Soon</u>

BONDED BY BLOOD 2

BOW DOWN TO MY GANGSTA